# Amos Daragon

## THE KEY OF BRAHA

Don't miss

AMOS DARAGON #1: *The Mask Wearer*

# Amos Daragon

## THE KEY OF BRAHA

*Translated from the French by Y. Maudet*

# BRYAN PERRO

## Delacorte Press

Translation copyright © 2012 by Y. Maudet
Jacket art copyright © 2012 by Allen Douglas

All rights reserved. Published in the United States by Delacorte Press, an imprint of Random House Children's Books, a division of Random House, Inc., New York. Originally published in paperback in French in Canada as *Amos Daragon La Clé de Braha* by Les Editions des Intouchables, Quebec, in 2003. Copyright © 2003 by Les Editions des Intouchables.

Delacorte Press is a registered trademark and the colophon is a trademark of Random House, Inc.

Visit us on the Web! randomhouse.com/kids

Educators and librarians, for a variety of teaching tools, visit us at randomhouse.com/teachers

Library of Congress Cataloging-in-Publication Data is available upon request.

ISBN 978-0-385-73904-7 (trade)
ISBN 978-0-385-90767-5 (lib. bdg.)
ISBN 978-0-375-89694-1 (ebook)

The text of this book is set in 12.5-point Goudy Old Style.
Book design by Trish Parcell

Printed in the United States of America
10 9 8 7 6 5 4 3 2 1
First American Edition

Random House Children's Books
supports the First Amendment and celebrates the right to read.

# Contents

# PROLOGUE

A long, long time ago, an imposing city rose amid the lux-
uriant lands of Mahikui. The city was called Braha, mean-
ing "divine marvel of the world" in the Mahite language.
A huge pyramid erected in the town center was enough to
justify the title of "marvel." The Mahites, a peaceful and
gentle people, lived there for centuries in tranquillity. Yet
one day the gods grew jealous of Braha's beauty and decided
to seize this precious gem. Combining their power, the gods
triggered a cataclysm that buried Braha. A huge sandstorm
covered the city, transforming neighboring lands into a
sterile desert. The "divine marvel of the world" took on
another dimension and became the entry harbor for all the
souls of the dead.

The city was given a new name: City of the Dead.

A grand tribunal was created to judge the newly arrived souls. There were two doors in the tribunal: one led to paradise, the other to hell. The only remnant of the former city was the tip of the pyramid, which stuck out of the desert sands. It was said that the gods had planted a fabulous tree there—a tree that bore fruits of light and had the power to elevate any mortal to the rank of a divinity. The following inscription was written on a metal door protected by two guards:

> *The one who dies and comes back to life,*
> *The one who sails the Styx*
> *And finds his way,*
> *The one who answers the angel*
> *And vanquishes the devil*
> *Is the one who will find the key of Braha.*

As time went by, this story became a legend. And little by little, from century to century, the legend grew blurred in men's memory.

# —1—

# THE CLOSING OF THE DOORS

Mertellus was seated at his desk. The specter flicked through a big law book. When he was alive, Mertellus had been one of the greatest judges the world had ever known. When he died, the gods chose him to preside over the grand tribunal of Braha, the City of the Dead. For five hundred years, Mertellus had gone to the tribunal every night. Together with Korrillion and Ganhaus, his peers, he judged the dead who came before him.

One by one, the deceased entered the court. The three judges carefully pondered each file before rendering their verdict. If the deceased had behaved badly in life, the door to hell was opened and a large staircase led him or her to the depths of Earth, where the negative gods dwelled. If the deceased had been filled with acts of goodness and compassion, the door leading to heaven and the positive gods was opened.

Most of the time, the three magistrates were unanimous in their decisions and the procedure was just a formality. But every so often a file presented some difficulties: there might be errors in the computing of good and bad actions; sometimes the soul of the deceased remained emotionally linked to the world of the living. Promises made before death and not kept could also impair the procedure, and to further complicate things, a divine damnation could be attached to the file.

At the slightest doubt, the deceased was returned to the City of the Dead, where, pending a new judgment, he or she was doomed to remain prisoner. Denied entry to either realm, the poor, anguished ghost wandered in the gigantic city—sometimes for decades. The City of the Dead was thus filled with specters waiting to be judged, and although Mertellus and his assistants worked relentlessly, they were unable to reduce the glut. Newcomers settled in Braha every day, and the problem of overpopulation was becoming acute.

Comfortably seated at his desk, Mertellus consulted the big law book to try to shed light on a difficult case. An ordinary man, neither good nor bad when alive, had refused to open his house to a woman who asked for shelter on a cold winter night. He found her dead, frozen on his doorstep, the next morning.

In the file, the gods of good asked for reparations for

the woman. They demanded that this callous human be condemned to haunt his own house until he could pay his debt to another person in need. But the gods of evil wanted him immediately in hell. They cited clause B124-TR-9, or the "determinant action" clause, which stipulated that all human beings were to be judged according to the weight of their heaviest sin. This clause contradicted clause G617-TY-23, or the clause of "daily goodness," which said humans were the sum of their many small acts of kindness, not of their sporadic aberrations. Discouraged, Mertellus was impatiently looking for a precedent. Around him, hundreds of files just as complicated as this one cluttered the tables, chairs, library shelves, and even windowsills, waiting to be solved.

Quite suddenly, Mertellus's office door opened and Jerik Svenkhamr entered. He was a petty thief who had been sent to the guillotine. Unable to put his head back on his shoulders, he always carried it in his hands or under his arm. He had been condemned to hell for the thefts he had committed but had refused to go. The god of justice, Forseti, had intervened on Jerik's behalf and suggested he serve a punishment of one thousand years doing the bidding of the tribunal. And so Jerik was appointed to serve Mertellus and became his personal secretary. Jerik was nervous and clumsy. He could not spell, which for one hundred and fifty-six years had driven the great judge to despair. Mertellus gave a jolt when Jerik came in.

"Jerik! Mean robber of little old ladies. I've told you one hundred times to knock before entering!" Mertellus shouted. "One day, you'll scare me to death!"

Panicked by his master's ire, the secretary tried to boost his self-confidence by putting his head back on his shoulders, but it toppled backward, falling heavily to the ground, where it rolled toward the stairs. The judge could hear Jerik's head shout as it hurtled down the steps.

"I can't . . . *ouch!* . . . kill you . . . *woo!* . . . You are . . . *aye!* . . . already . . . *ouch!* . . . dead! . . . *ouch!*"

Jerik ran after his head, but without his eyes, he fell on the steps, making an awful racket as he took down a good amount of armor decorating the staircase.

Mertellus sighed. "What have I done to deserve this?" he said, imploring the gods.

The only answer to his question was Jerik's timid voice as he reappeared in Mertellus's office, holding his head firmly in his hands and bowing ridiculously.

"Master Mertellus! Your Honor . . . no . . . I mean . . . enlightened judge of human destiny! Great decider in the name of the gods and . . . uh, wise man of the law and—"

The magistrate boiled with anger. "Can you tell me why you have to disturb me?" he shouted. "Come to the point, you stupid crook!"

Visibly terrified, Jerik tried to put his head back on his shoulders again. But the judge, who feared a repetition of the fall down the stairs, intervened.

6

"Jerik!" he said. "Come here and put your head on my desk. I want you to sit on the floor. Now!"

The secretary quickly obeyed.

"All right," the old ghost said as he looked the head straight in its eyes, "tell me what is going on or I will bite your nose off!"

Jerik swallowed hard. "The large doors are . . . I mean . . . how do I explain it? They are . . . uh . . . they are closed!"

The judge dealt him a blow on the head. "Be more precise!" he shouted. "Which doors?"

"Yes, there it is," the secretary answered. "Judge Korrillion and Judge Ganhaus, sent me to inform you that the doors . . . you know . . . the two doors . . . the ones leading to paradise and to hell . . . are . . . well . . . they are shut. I mean . . . uh . . . that no one can open them! The gods have blocked the doors! It's . . . a . . . uh . . . a catastrophe!"

Mertellus grabbed his secretary's head by the hair and quickly went down the stairs leading to the large tribunal room. Once there, with Jerik's head hanging from his hand, the judge understood how serious the situation was: he saw Korrillion pulling at his beard in desperation, while Ganhaus relentlessly kicked the doors. Both men were beside themselves.

"We're doomed!" Korrillion cried as he threw his arms around Mertellus. "The gods are against us. There are too many souls in the city. I have too many files to check. I can't cope any longer. Just can't cope."

"Bring me an ax!" Ganhaus shouted. "I swear I'm going to open these doors! An ax, I say!"

The magistrate carelessly tossed his secretary's head in a corner of the room and ordered his colleagues to calm down. Korrillion and Ganhaus eventually came to their senses. The three specters sat around a large oak table and Mertellus spoke.

"My friends! We are confronted with a situation that goes beyond our respective abilities," he began. "Korrillion, second magistrate, is right. The city is overflowing with ghosts, mummies, skeletons—in short, with too many souls awaiting judgment. If the only exits used to evacuate them are now closed, we will face public unrest. We must find a solution!"

A heavy silence filled the room. The three judges racked their brains.

"I may have a way," Ganhaus said finally. "I recall a story that I heard a very long time ago. It seems that there is a key to open these doors. Let me try to remember. Yes, the key would be hidden in the depths of the city. It would have been made especially in case a situation such as this one arose. It was . . . yes . . . it's coming back to me . . . it was at the time Braha was created, some thousands of years ago. The first magistrate of the City of the Dead had it made by a famous elf locksmith without the gods' knowledge."

"We're saved, then!" Korrillion exploded with joy. "Let's find this key and open the doors!"

Mertellus shook his head. "This story is probably nothing more than a groundless legend," he said. "We have no proof that this key really exists."

"You're right, it's not a good solution!" Ganhaus acknowledged. "What's more, if this story is true, the place where the key is kept is said to be guarded by two powerful forces that would stop whoever tries to enter. That would be another problem to solve. As I remember, the story stated that only a mortal can retrieve the key and activate the mechanism that opens the doors of good and evil."

Mertellus looked at Ganhaus skeptically. "How do you know all this?"

"My grandmother told me the story," Ganhaus answered. "She was a clairvoyant who could not control her visions. Throughout my childhood I was rocked to sleep with these fantastic tales. Of course, that was when I was alive, many years ago. My people, the gypsies, loved these kinds of morbid stories. My grandmother was no doubt a strange woman, but everybody respected her."

"Even if all this is true," Korrillion said, "what mortal would agree to sail the Styx, the river of death, to come to the help of a city of specters? No one would risk losing their life for the sake of a ghost! It's a well-known fact that the living are afraid of ghosts!"

Once again, a heavy silence filled the room. After a

few minutes, Jerik's head, which still lay unclaimed on the floor, spoke up.

"Huh . . . I heard your conversation and . . . I think . . . let's see . . . I think I know who could come to your aid."

The three judges looked at each other with incredulity. No one paid attention to the secretary, and silence resumed.

"As I just said, I . . . I can help you," Jerik insisted. "If one of you could . . . uh . . . I mean . . . pick my head up from under the chair over here, in the corner of the room, I'd be . . . uh . . . happy to share my idea with you."

There was no reaction from the judges. Scorning the secretary, the magistrates were still trying to find a solution.

"Anyone there?" Jerik asked in a hesitant voice. "Hello?"

With a shrug, Mertellus looked at his colleagues. The magistrates had nothing to lose. He rose and went to the corner of the room, grabbed Jerik's head, and set it on the table with a thud. He then returned to his seat.

"Go ahead!" he said. "We're all ears!"

Ganhaus leaned close to the secretary's face. "If it turns out that you're wasting our time," he threatened, "I'll throw you in the Styx!"

Worried, Jerik managed a timid smile. "Uh . . .well . . . do you remember, about a month ago, a sorcerer named Karmakas came before you?" he began. "You dispatched him to hell and—"

"Considering the number of files we have to deal with in a month, do you really believe that we can possibly remember every single case?" Korrillion asked, clearly irritated.

"Let me finish!" Jerik begged. "This sorcerer, a little crazy, I believe . . . could not stop railing against someone named Amos Daragon. He said . . . let's see . . . again and again . . . he repeated constantly: 'I'll get you, Mask Wearer. I'll kill you, Amos Daragon, and I'll reduce your brain to pulp.'"

"So what?" Mertellus shouted in exasperation.

"So," Jerik went on, "out of curiosity . . . uh . . . I did some research in a section of the library . . . the section where . . . how do I say this . . . ?"

"Where you're not supposed to go!" Ganhaus answered angrily. "Surely you mean the library that is forbidden to subordinates. I should say *formally* forbidden to people like you!"

Jerik began to sweat abundantly. Large drops formed on his forehead.

"Yes . . . uh . . . yes, yes, the very one. I entered there by chance, but that's another story . . . uh . . . and if you wish, we'll talk about it later. So, to come back to my research, I discovered that mask wearers are human beings chosen by the Lady in White to bring back . . . I mean . . . bring back some balance to the world. When the gods are at war . . . as is now the case . . . it's no secret . . . there are those . . . I mean the mask wearers, of course . . . who take over and watch that the equilibrium between . . . uh . . . good and evil is restored and . . . uh . . . give help to the victims of the gods' war.

"What we're going through now . . . if you'll allow me . . . is obviously . . . uh . . . a powerful imbalance! We should therefore try to find this Amos Daragon and ask for his help. The legend of the key is the only trail to a solution. We should follow it and put this . . . uh . . . great man in charge! What do you think?"

Mertellus was impressed by what he had just heard.

"I believe we have a plan," he declared. "One point remains to be clarified, though. Who is going to flush out this Amos Daragon and bring him here?"

After a few minutes of thought, the three magistrates directed their gaze to Jerik's head. It was obvious that he had just been designated to find Amos Daragon. He wanted to protest, but it was too late.

"I approve this choice," Ganhaus said, pointing his finger at the secretary.

"I second this proposition wholeheartedly," Korrillion added.

"Your wisdom is great, dear friends," Mertellus said. He laughed. "I approve your decision, and it's with great sadness that I'll part with such a good secretary." He turned to Jerik. "It's the moment of truth for you, my dear Jerik! If you succeed in your mission, I'll cancel your one-thousand-year sentence to serve the Justice Department and you will be sent to paradise. On the other hand, if you fail, you'll haunt hell till the end of time!"

Sniggering, the three judges got up. They had found a glimmer of a solution to their problem, as well as a scape-goat to do their dirty work.

"You'll leave tonight!" Mertellus said, turning to his secretary. "I'll advise Charon, the captain of the Styx riverboat. I'll also get in touch with Baron Samedi so he delivers you a boarding pass that you'll hand to this . . . this . . . Amos something! That way, he'll be able to reach us easily!"

Korrillion followed Mertellus out of the room. Only Ganhaus lingered.

"Perfect! You played your part very well!" he whispered with satisfaction to Jerik. "My two colleagues fell into the trap. When Seth frees my murderous brother Uriel from hell, we'll eliminate Amos Daragon, this mask wearer, and we'll have the key of Braha. If you fail in your mission, I swear you'll have a dear price to pay!"

The judge slammed the door on his way out. Jerik, whose head was right in the middle of the table, shuddered.

"I really have a knack for getting into binds!" he said softly. "Whatever the scheme, it's always I who . . . uh . . . does the dirty work! There is no justice in this world!"

# −2−

# THE SPECIAL ENVOY
# OF BARON SAMEDI

For the past few months, Amos Daragon had lived in the fortified city of Berrion. Along with his parents, Urban and Frilla, he occupied lavish apartments inside the castle. Junos, the lord of the realm, proudly provided them with shelter. Their adventure with the gorgons in Bratel-la-Grande had woven solid links between him and the Daragon family.

On a cool September morning, Amos was sleeping peacefully in his bedroom when his friend Beorf burst in.

"Get up, Amos!" the plump boy shouted excitedly. "Lord Junos wants to see you in the castle courtyard. Quick! Hurry up, it's important!"

Hardly awake, Amos got up and dressed rapidly. In haste, he combed his long hair, put on his wolf's-head earring, and adjusted his leather armor, a gift from his mother. The sun had barely risen when Amos arrived in the interior courtyard. The entire castle staff was gathered, eagerly awaiting the mask wearer. The inquisitive crowd had formed a circle around something or someone. The cooks were whispering together, while the guards, the knights, and the archers of the realm manned their lookout posts. The grooms seemed hypnotized and the servants were eyeing each other anxiously.

Beorf, too, was worried. He stood, ready for a fight, right by Junos's side. The lord and king of Berrion was still in his nightgown, looking perplexed and anxious. His yellow and green nightcap made him look silly, a little like an old clown. But all eyes were on the center of the courtyard. Amos made his way easily through the crowd, which opened a path for him. His parents saw him reach the dais where Lord Junos and Beorf were waiting.

Right away Amos understood what the matter was. In the center of the gathering were about twenty men, their backs ramrod straight, perfectly immobile. Their skin was as dark as night and their bodies were covered with brightly colored war paint. These fighters, who came from parts unknown, had shaved heads and wore huge jewels made of gold, precious stones, and animal bones. They were lightly dressed in animal skins, their powerful muscles and battle scars visible to all. Barefoot, with bloodshot eyes and pointed teeth, these men carried menacing spears on their backs. Close to them rested five black panthers, their tongues hanging out. Seeing this, Amos went closer to Junos.

"You wanted to see me, Junos?" he whispered. "What is going on?"

"No, not me!" the lord answered in a low, worried tone. "Our visitors arrived at the door of the city this morning asking for you. They are probably demons—be very careful! Look at the size of their cats. They're huge! If things take a bad turn, my knights are ready to attack. At the slightest sign of hostility, we'll quickly send these men back to hell!"

Amos turned toward Beorf and gave a quick nod. Beorf knew what was expected of him. The mask wearer's trusted companion was of the humanimal race, a man-beast, or beorite, who had the power to transform into a bear. He was round as a barrel, and his eyebrows met above his nose; he also had heavy blond sideburns, and hair covered the palms of his hands. Beorf stepped down from the dais with Amos, careful to stay back so that he could morph into a bear and spring into action if necessary.

"I am the one you wanted to see," Amos said, addressing the visitors.

The warriors looked at one another and slowly moved aside. Everyone then saw a young girl, about ten years old, at the center of the gathering. No one had noticed her before. She moved toward Amos with dignity. Her skin was the color of ebony. Her hair, very long and braided in hundreds of plaits, almost touched the ground. Sumptuous gold jewels circled her neck, waist, wrists, and ankles. Large bracelets, beautiful finely intertwined belts, cleverly carved necklaces, and numerous earrings of different shapes made her look like a princess. She was magnificent. An elongated jewel pierced her nostrils. She wore a black fur cape and a leopard-skin dress that left her belly button uncovered. Her navel was pierced as well, with a jewel made of green stone. The girl stopped in front of Amos and looked him straight in the eyes.

"I am Lolya, queen of the Dogon tribe," she told him. "I set off on a very long journey from my native land to meet you. Baron Samedi, my god and spiritual guide, appeared to me and ordered me to bring you a gift."

The queen snapped her fingers. One of the warriors came forward and placed a wooden box at the girl's feet. She opened it with care. Curiosity overcame fear, and the onlookers drew closer to see the mysterious gift.

"Take it!" Lolya declared, bowing with respect. "This object is now yours!"

Amos bent down over the box and took a magnificent mask out of it. The crowd beamed with admiration when they saw the beauty of the gift. It was made of pure gold and represented the face of a man whose beard and hair were the shape of flames.

"Are you really offering me this?" Amos asked, perplexed but dazzled by the mask. "It's marvelous."

"This mask has been in my family for . . . many

generations," the girl said hesitantly. "A long time ago, one of my ancestors was also a mask wearer. With this gift, I am offering you the power of fire. I hope you will use it well, as it is very precious. It won't be of any use without the power stones that go with it, but you already know this."

"Yes," Amos answered. "I'm wearing the mask of air. Only one stone is embedded in it. But it gives me some power over the wind."

"You're wearing it at this very moment?" the young queen asked.

"Yes. The mask fits completely onto my face and becomes invisible."

"Your quest is at its beginning. You still have to find two more masks and fifteen stones."

"But I'm only twelve!" Amos exclaimed. He laughed. "I still have a lot of time ahead of me."

"May I ask you something?" asked the queen of the Dogons.

"Yes, I'm listening."

"I know that my appearance, and that of my warriors, is not one you're accustomed to. It may frighten you. But we are here as friends. The Dogons are peaceful people; you have nothing to fear from us. As I told you, our journey was long and—"

"Of course! I understand that you must be tired," Junos interrupted. "Let me introduce myself! I am Junos, lord and king of Berrion. You are my guests. Let the best rooms

18

of the castle be given to them!" he ordered his servants. "Tonight we will hold a banquet to honor our guests! Let's prepare the feast. I will supervise the preparations. Knights, consider these visitors our friends! Perhaps they can teach us some of their songs and dances this evening. We'll also find a place to keep your giant cats. Knights of Equilibrium, let's hurry! Carry on!"

All the castle dwellers applauded. Their fear had dissipated. Amid this noisy demonstration of joy, Lolya decided to be less formal.

"I must to speak to you alone," she whispered to Amos. "It's terribly urgent—we have little time."

Amos nodded and said a few words in Beorf's ear. The humanimal ran off to ask Junos permission to use the castle's secret meeting room. Meanwhile, Amos and Lolya left the square unnoticed.

ᛘ

"We won't be disturbed here," Amos told Lolya.

They had used a secret passage that led directly to the meeting room of Junos and his Knights of Equilibrium. Only a privileged few knew that this room existed. Six chairs and a rectangular table were the only furniture. Beorf entered in the company of a servant who carried a huge basket filled with fruit, nuts, dried meat, and bread, which she placed at the center of the table. Beorf closed the passage door behind the servant and sat next to Amos.

19

Relieved, Lolya smiled. She threw her cape on the floor, took off her jewelry, undid her hair and gathered it in a huge bun at the back of her head. She then jumped onto the table, grabbed the basket between her legs, and began gobbling up food. Amos and Beorf were speechless. The girl was biting avidly into the fruit and filling her mouth with bread while emitting little cries of satisfaction. The sweet and precious young queen had turned into a famished animal wolfing down food.

"This, my dear friend, is the kind of girl I like!" Beorf said to Amos.

"Shall we?" asked Amos.

"Let's!" Beorf answered.

The two boys jumped on the table and, like Lolya, began to eat hungrily. Happy for the company, Lolya filled Amos's mouth with grapes while she ate nuts from her other hand. She even competed with Beorf to determine which of them was able to put the most food in their mouth. The humanimal won by a hair. For a while, the three had fun stuffing themselves, throwing food at each other, and burping noisily.

When the feast ended, Beorf fell from the table and rolled onto the floor. His stomach now full, he plunged into the deep sleep of a satiated bear. Meanwhile, Amos loosened his belt and sprawled out on a chair, arms dangling, both feet on the table. Lolya stretched out on the table among the leftover fruit and nutshells.

"I was so hungry!" she said to Amos. "You can't imagine! I've had nothing to eat for a week. My warriors and I had no provisions left. Today I ate like a queen! I have not had such a good time in a long while. I'm eleven years old and very tired of being queen. I've governed my people since the death of my parents. I'm not supposed to laugh, play, or do silly things. I hate formalities, and the—"

Lolya stopped talking and raised her head to hear better.

"Do you hear that noise, Amos?" she asked. "What is it? It sounds like a growling animal!"

"Don't be afraid, it's only Beorf's snoring," Amos answered, laughing.

"It's horrible! Does he always make so much noise when he sleeps?"

"That's nothing. In a few minutes, we won't be able to hear ourselves talk!" Amos said, laughing even more.

The young girl turned over onto her stomach and crawled toward Amos. She put her head on her folded arms.

"Let's talk seriously now," she said, "though I don't know where to begin! You must know that there are several types of magic?"

"Indeed," Amos answered, "it's no secret."

"Mask wearers like you have power over the elements, isn't that so?" Lolya asked.

"That's correct," Amos confirmed. "As you know, there are four masks—one each for earth, water, air, and fire. But it is the stones that give the masks their real power."

The young queen nodded. "Well, I am able to harness

the energy of the dead," she said. "I practice a form of sorcery that in my country is called voodoo. I can bewitch people, create zombies, and cast good or bad spells, but I excel at communicating with spirits. My spiritual guide, Baron Samedi, is a god. Through him, I know that the world of the dead is trying to get in touch with you. Someone wants to communicate with you. That is why I am here. I must, with my powers, unlock a door for you that opens onto the world of the invisible."

As he listened to Lolya, Amos grew serious again.

"Do you know anything more?" he asked, puzzled. "Is this all Baron Samedi told you?"

"That's all I know," answered the young girl. "He appeared to me in a vision asking that I give you the mask of fire. Then he guided me to you in my dreams. My guards and I traveled through several countries and faced huge dangers to find you. Soon I will be able to open this door for you, but . . . for the time being . . . Wait, don't move, let me get my jacks."

Lolya climbed off the table, picked up her cape from the ground, and took a small multicolored bag out of it. The young queen came back to sit near Amos and opened the bag. Seven strange-looking little bones fell out of it.

"Close your eyes, Amos," she said. "I'll try to read your future."

The Dogon queen placed her thumbs over Amos's eyes and put her forehead against his. Amos felt a wave of warmth come over him. As Lolya concentrated and uttered some incomprehensible words, he began to relax. The girl moved away suddenly, took the jacks in one hand, and threw them hard against a wall while howling more magic words. Then she calmed down.

"Look, Amos," she said, pointing to the jacks on the ground. "Their position shows me several things. Soon you will face a plot against you. Someone wants to use you to bring this world to an end. I see that you will be unable to use your new powers to overcome your enemies. Your sharp mind will be your best weapon. You will also have to listen to your heart to go . . . wait . . . yes, to go meet a tree. You will have to be wary of everyone, even me. I see a bad event occurring during this adventure: you will lose a friend. This person will sacrifice himself so you can accomplish your mission."

Amos was shaken by the prediction. "Do you know this friend's name?" he asked.

"No. I only know that it is someone you love dearly. Someone very close to you."

Amos remained silent. His and Lolya's eyes went to Beorf, who was snoring innocently.

# —3—

## THE CEREMONY

Lolya and her warriors had been at the castle for almost a week. The Dogon delegation had adapted quite well to the customs of the Berrion, but their presence was the source of many rumors and gossip.

The people of Berrion were suspicious of the war paint that covered the visitors, and they spread slanderous and preposterous stories about the Dogon warriors and their young queen. The most narrow-minded gossipers said that the warriors were devils sent to Earth to take their city. That it was the fire of hell that had turned their skin black, to give them a distinctive mark.

Junos had dispatched his public speaker to inform his subjects of the presence of these prestigious guests. He had also demanded that the population treat the warriors with dignity. But it is more difficult to open an obtuse mind than a heavily defended fortress; very few people had taken his message into account. Mothers forbade their children to leave home. Men met in taverns to devise plans to get rid of the strangers.

The Dogons sensed the apprehension and hostility as they walked through the city, and decided to remain in the castle. This decision increased the rumors; in every street, in every house, and in the marketplace, it was said that these people were now secretly governing Berrion and that Lord Junos, bewitched by their powerful magic, had signed an agreement with the gods of evil for the destruction of his people. To prevent the escalation of collective fear, Junos had to walk the city every day to reassure his citizens. All his friendly words about the Dogons were misinterpreted. And so every day, the lord returned to the castle in a desperate and anguished state of mind. An uprising was hatching and the citizens of Berrion were losing faith in their lord.

"What can I do?" Junos asked after explaining the predicament to Amos. "I know that you're young, but even at twelve you're wiser than most of my white-bearded advisors. I can feel that I'm losing control of the situation. I need your help. I have to please my people, but I cannot send our guests away. I offered them hospitality, and when I give my word, I never take it back."

"A solution has to be found quickly," Amos answered.

"For three days I've tried to speak to Lolya, but she refuses to come out of her room. She's not eating. I don't know what's going on. A few hours ago I caught her eating stones in the castle courtyard before she disappeared into her room. She looked like a ferocious animal. She was talking to herself, repeating the name Kur. I don't know who that is. She was talking as if Kur were here. When I put my hand on her shoulder, she pushed me back rudely and growled. I haven't seen her since.

"All the Dogon warriors look fine, although their queen seems sick. I asked Beorf to watch the door to her room. I don't know what to do either, Junos." Amos sighed. "During our first meeting, Lolya mentioned her spiritual guide, Baron Samedi, for whom she said she had to do something. Apparently, the world of the dead wants to get in touch with me. What's more, she predicted what sounded like Beorf's death.

"She also said that I should be wary of her. I don't know what to make of all this. I have a bad feeling about it, and I confess that I have some doubts about Lolya. It's as if she has two personalities."

"Do you know, Amos, that she chased after one of my cooks with a big knife?" Junos admitted. "She wanted to kill him for treason. She was shouting that he had the evil eye. I don't know what that means, but it took three of my men to keep her from killing him. She is strong when she's angry. A real beast!"

Amos nodded. "My father once told me a story about three fish that were swimming quietly in a lake when they noticed the net of a fisherman. The first fish understood the danger and left immediately. Carefree, the other two soon found themselves prisoners in the net. One of them immediately floated belly-up, playing dead. The fisherman wanted to bring back fresh food to his family, so he took that fish and threw it on the shore. The fish used its tail to propel itself back into the water and saved its life. The third fish was unable to foresee its fate and ended up in the fisherman's frying pan. The moral of this story is simple: those who are not perceptive or clever enough in the face of danger always end up in the clutches of their enemy."

"Well," Junos said, "I don't trust this girl at all, even if she is a queen. Imagine! She cuts the throat of chickens to read the future in their entrails. Twice she did this in front of my servants before locking herself in her room. One of my maids reported it to me."

Amos raised his head to the starry sky. He and Junos were in the castle courtyard.

"Something tells me that we're going to hear from Lolya tonight," Amos said. "Look, Junos, it's a full moon, and the stars are particularly bright. I also have a premonition that I'm about to die."

At that moment, Beorf arrived. He was out of breath and very excited.

"She came out of her room!" he shouted. "Lolya is walking toward the city with her men!"

Amos, Beorf, and Junos rushed out of the castle. In the marketplace, Lolya and her warriors had already lit a big fire. The Dogons, dressed in tiger skins and wearing fresh war paint, gathered around the fire and began to play some music. They had big drums and a lot of smaller percussion instruments. The people of Berrion, armed with rakes, shovels, and picks, cautiously moved closer to this strange assembly.

The sound of tom-toms slowly rose. Lolya, barefoot and close to the fire, began to dance. She wore a yellow ceremonial dress and carried a large knife in her belt. White makeup covered her face. From a distance, she looked like a skull. Junos ordered his knights to be on the ready to contain the crowd or calm his guests. Amos and Beorf looked at each other, not sure what to do. The percussion grew louder and the queen danced faster.

"To come back to your fish story," Junos said as he bent toward Amos. "I believe that the net has been thrown and that it is too late to escape. I'm counting on your clever ways to get us out of this situation, my friend."

"All I have to do is play dead," Amos said ironically.

Soon the rhythm of the drums filled the marketplace. The dance of the young queen hypnotized the spectators. No one was able to move. The people of Berrion, as well as the knights, watched the show totally motionless. All willpower had deserted them; the bewitching sound of the instruments was rooting them to the soil. And then, for no apparent reason, the entire population of the city started to thump the ground. Prisoner of the music, each person began to move slowly. The sound penetrated minds and bodies. Lolya jumped, cried, and danced faster and faster.

A dark veil covered the bright full moon. Amos, almost completely under the spell of the dance, decided that it was a lunar eclipse. Beorf danced by his side, half man, half bear. The rotund boy was beside himself with agitation. Those around the mask wearer seemed to have lost their minds. As Junos waved his arms wildly in the air, several of his knights rolled on the ground.

When the moon disappeared, Lolya suddenly ended her dance and pointed her finger toward Amos. An incomprehensible force drew Amos through the crowd, and he joined the queen in the middle of the circle of Dogons, near the big fire. Lolya ceremoniously took her knife out of its sheath. The drums fell silent. The spell was broken and everyone stopped dancing. As the crowd was slowly coming back to their senses, Lolya ferociously knifed Amos in his abdomen.

"The door is open!" she shouted.

A strong burning sensation shot through the mask wearer. Frilla Daragon cried in horror when she saw her only son fall to the ground. Amos heard his heartbeats slow down, become weaker and weaker—until they stopped.

The knights rushed toward the Dogons to prevent any move on their part. The warriors and their queen offered no resistance. Urban Daragon hurried to his son, while Junos stood paralyzed by the spectacle.

"I should—I should have expected this. I should have known . . . ," he stammered.

In tears, Frilla ran to join her husband. Urban cried in front of Amos's still body, then looked up at Frilla.

"He's dead!" he declared with deep sorrow. "Our son is dead!"

At that moment, the powerful and mad howling of a young bear rang out. With a vigorous leap forward, Beorf threw himself at Lolya and pinned her to the ground.

"That was the only way to make him go across," the young queen managed to say as Beorf was about to strangle her. "He is not really dead . . . trust me!"

Beorf closed his powerful jaws just as the moon reappeared in the sky.

"Take them to jail!" Junos shouted. "And put the queen in solitary confinement! Tie her up!"

The man-bear loosened his grip and changed back to his human form. "I'll make you pay for this," he said into Lolya's ear. "Count on it!"

# —4—

## THE STYX

A strong scent of flowers woke Amos. He sneezed violently and opened his eyes. As he looked about, he realized that he was lying in a rectangular box. Around him lay roses, daffodils, lilies, and a few carnations. He raised his head a little and saw his father's and mother's faces. His parents were bent over him, crying their eyes out. Junos was standing right behind them, his eyes equally red and feverish.

Rising up a bit more, Amos saw Beorf. He was seated on the ground, his back against a tombstone. The plump boy was looking at the sky in a pensive way. His lips were moving. It looked as if he were talking to someone who wasn't there. Dozens of people Amos knew well walked here and there in the cemetery of Berrion. The mask wearer sat up, suddenly understanding that everyone had gathered in his honor. The rectangular box was a coffin, and he would soon be buried.

"They all think I'm dead!" Amos said to himself. "Yet I never felt so well in my whole life!" He stood up in the coffin. "Sorry, everybody, but my funeral is not today!"

The people gathered around him did not react. No one seemed to have heard him.

"I'm here, I'm not dead!" Amos went on, increasingly concerned. "Is this a joke? Father! Mother! I'm here, I'm alive!"

The people around him kept acting as if he weren't there. Stepping out of the coffin, Amos saw his own body in the wooden box. It gave him a jolt and he cried out. Incredulous, he looked again, more closely this time. It was definitely his body. He clearly saw his long braids and his earring in the shape of a wolf's head. He was dressed in the black leather armor that his mother had made for him, and his hands were crossed over his chest.

Then he remembered the ceremony with Lolya—the dance, the fire, the lunar eclipse, and the drums of the Dogons. He remembered the young queen's knife and re-lived his death. When he raised his eyes to look around, the mask wearer noticed that the landscape was not quite the same as before. The color of the trees was paler, more subdued, and the sky was a light gray. His body was slightly transparent, like that of a ghost. Lifting his hand, Amos tried to raise the wind. Nothing happened. He tried again. Still nothing. Amos no longer had any powers.

*Well,* he thought, *Lolya's prediction seems to have come true!*

The young queen had told him: "I see that you will be unable to use your new powers to overcome your enemies. Your sharp mind will be your best weapon."

Amos ran toward Beorf and put his arms around his friend's shoulders.

"Beorf, I'm here, I'm not dead! Listen, Beorf, my mind is alive. I don't know what world I'm in and I don't know what I'm supposed to do. Go and ask Lolya to—"

Tears welled in Beorf's eyes and he got up suddenly. Without paying any attention to Amos's words, he walked in the direction of the coffin. Amos tried to stop him, but Beorf easily passed through the mask wearer's ghostly body.

Amos ran after him. "Remember, Beorf!" he shouted. "I can't really be dead! I told you what Lolya said about my new mission. Listen to me! Stop, Beorf, and listen!"

The young humanimal leaned over the coffin to take a last look at his friend. The grave diggers had arrived. During the memorial ceremony, Junos had recounted his first and last adventures with Amos. He spoke of the events of Bratel-la-Grande, emphasizing the clever battle they had fought against the gorgons and the basilisk. He also mentioned the woods of Tarkasis, their visit with the fairies, and how Amos had been able to give him back his youth.

As Beorf contemplated Amos's body, the tribute rendered by the lord to his best friend rang in his ears.

Unforgettable memories flooded Beorf. Again he saw Amos confront Yaune the Purifier; he saw his friend triumph in the game of truth. Beorf felt very lonely, and his thoughts drifted to Medusa, the most beautiful of all gorgons. She was dead too. The humanimal's throat tightened as his eyes filled with tears again. At his side, Amos was still trying to communicate with him.

"Let me explain, Beorf. Lolya told me that the world of the dead wanted to get in touch with me. She also told me that she would have to open a door. Listen to me, for heaven's sake, make an effort! What's happening now is part of her plan, Beorf! Do you remember, after our first meal together, Lolya talked to me about a different type of magic?" He sighed. "But of course you don't, you were asleep. You always fall asleep at the wrong time!"

They were closing the coffin now. Amos panicked as he watched the grave diggers nail the lid shut. Frilla Daragon started to sob in her husband's arms. The mask wearer tried in vain to communicate with his parents. He tried to use his power over the wind to communicate through a sphere of air. Nothing. His magic didn't work. His soul was now in another dimension and air didn't obey him anymore. Amos shouted, jumped up and down, and tried to knock over a few tombstones. Still nothing. His parents and friends stood motionless, watching the grave diggers fill the hole. Amos witnessed his own burial, unable to intervene.

Amos followed Beorf as the crowd left the cemetery to go back to the city. He kept talking to Beorf, asking him repeatedly to question Lolya. But Beorf didn't hear a word. Not when Amos shouted in his ears, kicked him, or called him names. Beorf simply continued to cry silently. As he and Amos were about to pass the cemetery gates, Amos was hurled backward. A force field kept him inside. Surprised and upset, he tried again—unsuccessfully.

Desperate, Amos tried to keep Junos from leaving. He grabbed a shovel that lay against a wall and dealt the lord of Berrion a violent blow. But in Amos's hands, the shovel became transparent and vaporous. Junos didn't feel a thing. With a profound feeling of powerlessness, the young mask wearer watched his parents and friends disperse. He was a prisoner of the cemetery, and all he could do was go back to his tomb, where the two grave diggers were gathering their tools.

Amos stood a long time near his tomb, not knowing what to do next. He thought about what Lolya had told him, of the things she had predicted. That he would have to face his next quest without the use of his powers. That he would have to listen to his heart to make decisions. That at the end, one of his friends would die. Amos had a hard time understanding this jumble of predictions.

As he was trying to put some order to his thoughts, his eyes fell on a river flowing right in the center of the cemetery. Surprised, he approached the shore to make sure he wasn't hallucinating. No, it really was a river! He had never seen it when he had been alive. It looked very deep and dark. A horrible stench rose from it. The water flowed slowly, like a thick soup. Huge green bubbles regularly broke to the surface and let out fumes. Amos noticed an embankment close by that looked much like the one in his birthplace in the realm of Omain. The fishermen there had used it for the boarding and landing of passengers.

Amos walked along the embankment. At its end, he noticed a long cord hanging from a bell.

*I have nothing to lose at this point,* he thought. *Why not ring the bell and wait? I might attract somebody's attention!*

The sound of the bell resonated through the cemetery and then silence resumed. Amos tried again. Nothing. Discouraged, he turned to go back to the shore. A strong wind suddenly rose. Looking back, Amos saw a huge three-masted boat—almost as wide as the river—hurtling toward him.

The boat was in pitiful shape. Her hull had been pierced by dozens of cannonballs and appeared ready to break apart. Battle scars, soot, and blood covered the old war vessel. The sails were torn, the central mast was broken halfway up, and the mermaid figurehead had lost its head. The ghostly craft slowed down and stopped in front of Amos. Two skeletons jumped onto the embankment to moor the boat.

*I think I really succeeded in attracting the attention of . . . someone!* Amos thought, paralyzed with fear.

Like good sailors, the skeletons steadied the boat. They stood at attention, ropes in hand, facing the boy. A gangway fell in front of Amos, and a sinister-looking old man, dressed in rags, came down it.

"Your name?" he shouted.

"Amos . . . Amos Daragon, sir."

The gray-skinned and green-lipped old man took a thick leather book out of a bag. He looked through its pages for a few seconds.

"What's your name again?" he shouted impatiently.

"Amos Daragon."

"I can't find your name," the man hollered. "Scram, you little gnat. You're not dead."

As the captain was about to go back on board, Amos saw another man come down the gangway. He seemed nervous, and Amos was startled to see that he carried his head under his arm. The man approached the captain.

"I have an order . . . I mean . . . a letter from Baron Samedi to ensure . . . how should I say? . . . to ensure the boarding of Mr. Daragon. Take a look!"

"Very well," the old man whispered after reading the letter. "This paper clearly states that you are dead," he shouted to Amos. "My name is Charon and I'll be your captain for the duration of this trip. You must pay your fare now!"

"But I don't have any money," Amos answered.

The man who held his head under his arm came forward.

"Good day, Mr. Daragon. My name is Jerik Svenkhamr and I'm here to make sure that . . . I mean . . . that you have a safe trip to Braha. Look there . . . under your tongue . . . uh . . . in your mouth, surely there is a coin hidden there? Often people . . . how do I say this . . . often people leave a bit of money there to pay Master Charon for his services. It's an old tradition in several cultures!"

Amos put his fingers in his mouth. To his astonishment, he found a gold earring. He recognized it as one of Lolya's jewels. The young queen had probably slipped the earring under his tongue during the ceremony by the fire.

Amos didn't understand how he could have kept this jewel in his mouth without being aware of it. He handed it to Charon.

"Thank you," the captain said, laughing. "Make the most of your last trip!"

"Come, Master Daragon, come!" Jerik said, taking the mask wearer by the arm. "I thought you would be . . . uh . . . older, heavier . . . I mean . . . more adult."

"Can you explain to me what's going on?" Amos asked Jerik as they climbed the gangway. He was surprised to be addressed as "master." "I need to understand."

"Well . . . it's rather simple. I've been looking for you a long time. In fact, it's my master, Mertellus . . . uh . . . who wants to meet you. Right now we're on the river of death, the one called the Styx. You've met . . . the captain, Charon. As for me, I'm Mertellus's secretary. . . . I'm a former thief who was beheaded. It shows . . . uh . . . does it not?" He laughed. "Mertellus is the first magistrate of Braha . . . I mean . . . the first magistrate of the City of the Dead. How do I say this? . . . You will have to find a key that only a living human being can obtain, but the problem is that we don't know for sure if it exists! In any case, you're dead . . . but you'll have to come back to life! Do you see? Any questions? There is also Baron Samedi, without whom none of this would be possible! He's the one who sent Lolya to you. . . . Is all this clear?"

"I didn't understand a word of what you just said, Jerik," Amos answered, totally confused.

"I may not be the best person to . . . well . . . you see? I've lost my head somewhat. . . . Ha! . . . It's a joke. Well . . . in any case, it's true that I never had much of a head to begin with!"

The boat cast off. Amos sighed as the cemetery of Berrion slowly disappeared behind him.

# —5—

## LOLYA'S REVELATIONS

Order had been restored to the city of Berrion. Junos had apologized to his people. He had recognized his lack of common sense and his gullibility, and the citizens of Berrion had forgiven him. They all knew that the lord of the realm had a good heart, and no one mentioned this sad story of revolt again.

The Dogons had been jailed before Amos's funeral. After five days of mourning, Junos summoned the young queen to the palace courtyard. Since the extent of her magical power was not known, her feet and hands were chained when she was brought before the lord. In a very dignified way, Lolya bowed to the public, which hurled insults at her. Junos demanded silence.

"Lolya, queen of the Dogons," he said, "we welcomed

you and your men in this realm as friends. You betrayed our confidence! We don't put murderers to death, but you will pay dearly for killing my friend Amos Daragon. I sentence you to be taken to the fairies of the woods of Tarkasis. You will enter the forest as a child and come out of it as old as a grandmother."

"You seem to believe that I really killed Amos Daragon," Lolya said, denying the accusation.

"We saw you kill him!" Beorf shouted, outraged. "His heart stopped beating."

"He is not dead!" Lolya answered forcefully. "Listen to me carefully, because if you don't act now, your friend may lose his soul. It is difficult to explain. I'm following Baron Samedi's orders. He is my guide—"

"I've heard enough!" Junos cried. "Take her to the woods of Tarkasis! Afterward we will escort her warriors to the outskirts of the realm. I don't trust this little liar, who—"

Suddenly Lolya fell to the ground, where her body began to convulse. No one dared to move, worried that this might be another of her tricks. Her eyes turned inside out and foam formed on her lips; the young girl's body shook intensely as she uttered discordant sounds. The fit lasted for more than a minute. When she came back to herself, the young queen slowly got to her feet and wiped her mouth.

"Stupid humans!" she said in a strangely deep voice. "You don't know how to listen and you trust everything that your simplistic perceptions make you believe."

"What is this magic?" Junos demanded. "Seize her!"

Lolya burst out laughing. When two knights tried to grab her, their hands burned as they touched her skin. The two men ran toward the fountain in the courtyard, shouting with pain.

"No one can take hold of Baron Samedi!" the young queen said, smiling nastily.

She raised her arms and put the chain that imprisoned her hands in her mouth. In front of the disbelieving crowd, she crushed it like a nutshell between her teeth. Through willpower alone, she melted the metal links that bound her feet.

"Listen to me, Lord Junos!" Lolya said in a devilish voice. "Or I will broil all your knights."

As she pronounced these words, the armor of every knight became burning hot. Knives and swords took on the color of metal heated by a forge fire. The men began to run in every direction while trying to remove their armor. Some in the crowd tried to flee, but the castle doors were also intensely hot.

"Stop this nonsense!" Junos shouted. "I'm listening to you!"

"Very well," Lolya answered, and she canceled the spell. "You see Lolya before you, but she is not really here anymore. I use her body to talk to you. I am Baron Samedi, an ancient god of an ancient world you do not know. I have several names and several forms, and my powers are great."

"What do you want from of us?" Beorf hurled the question in challenge.

"There is one who is not afraid of death!" the baron said. "Your eyes show the same courage as your father and mother, young beorite. The man-bears are powerful and proud. I am the one who greeted your parents in the world of the dead when they were burned alive by Yaune the Purifier."

"I am glad to hear it," Beorf answered with arrogance and disdain. "Talk now and go back to where you come from!"

The young girl smiled and Baron Samedi went on. "Calm down! Amos Daragon, Mask Wearer, is not really dead. Following my orders, Lolya sent him to another dimension. Be kinder with this child! No more chains and no more jail! She is endowed with a vital strength. Her journey to Berrion has been long and difficult; half of her men died on the way. I made the mask of fire that she gave to Amos. There has never been a mask wearer in her family or among the Dogons. Lolya lied to you because she could not reveal our true motives, and because she wanted you to trust her. As I asked her to, she sent Amos Daragon to Braha, the great City of the Dead. I need him to settle an urgent matter. I also need you!

"I will tell you now what you have to do to bring Amos Daragon back to life. Exhume his body as soon as possible and take it to the desert of Mahikui. There, in the middle of this sea of sand, you will find a pyramid of which only the tip emerges from the ground. You will have to go through a door; Lolya will know how to activate the mechanism that opens it. In the center of this pyramid, you will leave the body of the mask wearer. Lolya will guide you along the way. The boy's body must be in place when the next eclipse of the sun happens, in exactly two months. You have no time to waste.

"Several of you will die during this undertaking. Be wary, Junos. Someone here, in this castle, wants to harm you. You are giving shelter to a spy. I am leaving now. Till we meet again!"

Baron Samedi's spirit left Lolya's body then, and she fell unconscious to the ground. Beorf morphed into a bear and ran swiftly to the cemetery. He was furiously digging at the earth when his adoptive parents, Urban and Frilla Daragon, joined him. In a few minutes, Amos's body was exhumed. The trio brought Amos back to the castle, where Junos demanded that Lolya be cared for.

In the evening, when calm had returned, Beorf went to see the body of his friend. Amos had been placed in his room, on his bed. Covered with a white sheet, he appeared to be sleeping soundly.

Dozens of candles had been lit, and their dancing flames cast a soft light on the walls. Beorf sat on the bed and spoke gently to his friend.

"Hello, Amos," he said. "I don't know if you can hear

me, but I need to talk to you. When I was a child, my father told me the story of his village blacksmith. One day this blacksmith came to see the high priest. He was upset and asked the wise man to give him permission to leave the village and hide on top of the mountain. Apparently the blacksmith had seen Death in person, looking at him in a terrifying way. Refusing to die, he had chosen to flee in the hope of escaping his fate. The priest gave him his blessing and the blacksmith left in a hurry. He reached the top of the mountain. But exhausted by the trip, he tripped over a stone and broke his neck. Death appeared at his side. The dying blacksmith asked: 'Why did you torture me with a terrifying look when I saw you in the village? You knew I was going to die, so why make me suffer?' Death answered: 'You misinterpreted my look. It was filled not with anger but rather with surprise. Yesterday I was told to go and get you on the mountain. So when I saw you in your forge, in the village, I wondered: *But how could this blacksmith be on the mountain when he is in the village, busy as can be, and perfectly happy? He has no reason to leave!*'"

Beorf sighed. "It seems, Amos, my friend, that we cannot escape our destiny. Baron Samedi told me that we are to meet again. As in my father's story, I just saw Death for the first time. I'm afraid to die, Amos."

As he finished, Beorf noticed a shadow in the corridor. Slowly, he went to the door, which was ajar, and spotted one of the castle's cooks going down the stairs furtively.

He recognized the man; it was the cook Lolya had chased with a knife in the palace kitchen. The young queen had accused him of treason and said that he had the evil eye. Beorf followed him to the stables. Before Beorf could stop him the cook stole a horse and rode off. Without hesitation, Beorf changed into his bear form and went after the fugitive.

*If my destiny is to die on this adventure,* he thought, *I'll die proudly, like my father and my mother! I'll not flee in front of danger!*

# —6—

## ON THE ROAD TO BRAHA

For a few hours now, Amos had tried to understand what Jerik was saying. The secretary had put his head on one of the boat barrels so as to give his arm a rest.

"Let me get this straight, Jerik," Amos said. "First, we are sailing the Styx, the river of death. This river flows in another dimension and the living cannot see it. Is that right?"

"Yes, that's quite right!" Jerik exclaimed. "Just as the key of Braha opens doors! Alive, it's possible! But dead . . . it is not! That's what I was saying—"

"One thing at a time," Amos said, cutting him short. "The souls of all the dead take this boat to reach a large city named Braha. Cemeteries are just boarding ports. Charon is the captain of this boat; his job is to collect the souls and bring them to Braha to be judged. The city is populated entirely by phantoms. Ghosts, like you and me, waiting to be sent to paradise or to hell. Three magistrates decide who goes to the world of positive gods and who goes to the world of negative gods, correct?"

"Precisely . . . you've got it all, except for the key, of course!" Jerik answered.

"I'm getting there. You, Jerik, work for Mertellus. There are two other judges, Ganhaus and Korrillion. One morning, without any warning, the two exit doors closed. It was impossible to open them. So you chose me to come to your rescue. I'm the one who has to find the key to get you out of this mess! Am I still right?"

"Exactly! But there is one more problem . . . to explain . . . I mean . . . rather, to settle. . . . As I was saying . . . a soul cannot—"

The boat stopped abruptly and Amos interrupted Jerik.

"You'll talk to me about this problem later," he said. "Let's go see what's going on!"

The souls of four or five fellow passengers followed Amos toward the gangway. They had reached the shores of a very small cemetery covered with flowers. Charon was refusing to take a family on board. The man was begging for the captain's mercy.

"Please, I only have this one coin to offer you! My three children, my wife, and I died when our cottage burst into flames," the man pleaded. "We're only peasants and have little money. We were a very united family in life. Please, don't separate us in death. . . ."

"Out of the question!" Charon shouted. "One coin per person! It's the law! Five people, five coins!"

"But I've nothing else to pay you with!"

"That's too bad!" the old captain shouted. "Your children and your wife will become wandering souls who will never find rest!"

Amos felt that he could not abandon this family to such a fate, so he pleaded on their behalf.

"Captain! Allow this family to come aboard." He tried to reason with Charon. "If this man has nothing to pay their fare, well, I'll pay it for him. In fact, if you allow them on the boat, I'll offer you twice nothing!"

Charon's eyes narrowed. "Very well," he said. "I gather that you want to trick me, young man. Well, if you don't give me exactly twice nothing, I'll throw you overboard! Agreed?"

"Agreed!" Amos answered with a large smile.

The family came on board. The man thanked Amos warmly. The father and mother and their three children snuggled up in a corner, waiting for what was to come next. In the meantime, Jerik approached Amos.

"You probably don't know . . . but . . . how do I say it . . . any soul that touches the Styx is automatically . . . uh . . . dissolved for eternity . . . reduced to nothing," he told Amos. "Since I need you in Braha . . . I think . . .

that . . . uh . . . this intervention is not a good idea! Charon will want to see his 'twice nothing' . . . and, well . . . I don't think that 'nothing' is really something . . . visible . . . much less palpable!"

"It all depends on how you look at things," Amos answered calmly as the captain approached them.

"Now pay me, Mr. Daragon!" Charon shouted. "I demand exactly twice nothing!"

"Right away," Amos said. "That big leather book in your bag, please—put it on the table, here."

"Why?" the captain asked.

"Do it and I will give you exactly what I owe you," Amos answered politely.

Charon grumbled but complied.

"Now, lift this big book and tell me what is underneath!" Amos said once the book was on the table.

"But . . . there is nothing!" Charon yelled.

"So, since you saw it, take it, it is all yours! Do it again and you will have exactly what I promised you: twice nothing. But please do not ask for more. I already promised three times nothing to somebody else!"

The two skeleton sailors tried to hide a smile. All the passenger souls burst out laughing. For the first time in his life as captain, Charon also had a hint of a grin on his face. The old man came close to Amos.

"You're quick-witted, young man! From now on, I'll keep an eye on you!" he said.

"At your service, Captain. And make good use of what I gave you!" Amos answered with a wink.

Taken aback by the turn of events, Jerik let himself fall slowly to the deck.

"I can't believe my eyes. . . . I thought things were going to end right here! On the Styx! You accomplished the impossible, Master Daragon. . . . You made Charon smile! In front of my eyes . . . he really smiled! You are definitely the one we need in Braha, Master Daragon! You make miracles happen!"

"Thank you for the compliment," Amos answered, pleased with himself.

A few days had gone by since Amos departed from Berrion.

He was bored. Always sailing the Styx, the boat often stopped to take on new passengers in the cemeteries along her route. This was how Amos became acquainted with a strange person, a scholar who cried bitterly as he boarded the ship. He was pitiful. After a few hours, the man opened up.

He had acquired his vast learning at the cost of incalculable hours of study. He knew the language, as well as the customs, of every country and spoke about the stars as if he had visited them, and no plant held any secret from him. He was a master in geography and history, yet he had never traveled. Everything he knew came out of books. From his very first years till the age of forty, the town library had been his only shelter.

At that point, knowing everything about the world, the man decided to take his first trip. He embarked on a boat that was to take him to a new continent. Sure of himself and of his knowledge, he asked the captain, who was a simple and frail man, whether he had studied grammar. The captain answered that he had not.

"Mathematics, perhaps?"

"No."

Anxious to show off his intellectual superiority, the learned man insisted, "Astronomy?"

"No."

"Alchemy?"

"No."

"Rhetoric?"

"No," the sailor answered respectfully.

"Well," the learned man said, "you've wasted your life, old man!"

Upset and distracted, the captain made a steering error and hit a reef. The boat's hull ripped; it began to sink. The captain looked at the learned man, who was as white as snow and clearly frightened.

"Tell me, since you know everything, surely you've learned to swim?" the old man asked.

"No, I cannot swim," the learned man confessed.

"Well," the captain went on, "I think that you're the one who wasted his whole life."

The old captain swam to shore and let the scholar sink with the boat. Charon's ship had collected the scholar's soul, cold and drenched, on the bank of the Styx. The learned man's name was Uriel of White-Earth. As the days went by, he became friendly with Amos and Jerik.

As Amos was killing time playing cards with Jerik and Uriel, one of the skeleton sailors tapped his shoulder. Amos turned around and saw the captain motion to him. He got up and followed Charon.

"What can I do for you?" Amos asked.

"Come to my cabin, you rascal!" the captain shouted.

Amos complied, even though he did not understand what was happening. Charon signaled to him to sit down. The captain remained standing and began to pace nervously around his small cabin.

"I want you to help me," Charon finally said. "I need you."

"What! You're no longer shouting, Captain?"

"No," Charon answered. "When I shout, it's to give off a certain bearing. My profession is a difficult one and my orders are strict. In no case am I supposed to show compassion toward my passengers. When I'm alone in my cabin, however, I confess that I cry about the children I have to abandon on the docks because they have no money. And then there are all the solitary souls, scared and powerless in death. I constantly have to shake these images out of my head. The stricter I show myself to be, the more I have to smother my true feelings. From the moment you boarded

53

this ship, I knew that you were different and that I could trust you. That is why I am telling you all this."

"Speak to me, I am listening," Amos said. "I am touched by your gesture and I will do all I can to help you."

"Here we go, then," Charon began. "I have been sailing this boat for centuries. I've seen all sorts of things and had lots of hard times! Yet there is one thing that I cannot get out of my head, something that keeps haunting me. Soon we will reach a large island where the inhabitants have been cast off for nearly three hundred years. They all died of thirst following a very serious drought caused by their god. He is a nasty god who still enjoys watching his followers suffer. He keeps them from boarding this boat. To be liberated from their torment of thirst, they have to solve a puzzle. It's very difficult, but I think you just might be smart enough to do it."

"What is this puzzle?" Amos asked.

"They have to make rain fall using only two jars of water," Charon answered, shaking his head. "It seems impossible to me, but . . . if it is a puzzle, there must be a solution."

"How can one make rain fall with two jars of water?" Amos said, perplexed.

"I do not know, or I would not have spoken to you about it!" the captain said, clearly getting impatient. "Please think about it," he added in a softer manner. "We will soon approach the island. If there is something you can do, then do it! If not . . . these wretched souls will continue to suffer till the end of time. And I will keep passing by the island, unable to change a thing."

Amos left the captain and headed out to rejoin Uriel and Jerik. The two men had been deep in conversation since Amos's departure.

"Seth set me free so that I would kill this boy," Uriel said. "Easy enough! And how is my brother, the great magistrate Ganhaus?"

"Good, good . . . he is fine . . . ," Jerik whispered. "I think Amos really believes that you are a scholar. You play your part well. Your story and . . . uh . . . your tears were truly credible! But we should not . . . how do I say . . . go too fast. You will kill Amos Daragon when he actually gets the key of Braha. Then you will give it to your brother."

"Believe me, I am patient! I'll do whatever is necessary," Uriel stated.

"Shush!" Jerik whispered. "Here he comes!"

Amos approached his travel companions. Noticing that he looked worried, Uriel pretended to be concerned.

"What's going on?" he asked. "Can we help you, my friend?"

"No," Amos answered. "It's between me and Charon. Come, let's go back to our game, if you don't mind."

"I have enough of my own problems, Master Daragon . . . and I mean . . . that they are rather complicated," Jerik said as he dealt the cards. "Wash your dirty linen within the family . . . as they say!"

Amos raised his eyes, looked at Jerik, and laughed. "Jerik, you just saved hundreds of souls from unending torment!" he said, and kissed the secretary on the forehead.

ψ

The gangway came down and Amos went ashore.

"I can give you one hour!" Charon shouted. "If you're not back, I'll have to leave you here!"

"Why is he going ashore?" asked Uriel, who did not want to lose sight of the young mask wearer.

"Mind your own business!" the captain hollered. "Play dead! I don't want to hear from you!"

"It would be difficult to be anything but dead on this boat," Uriel whispered viciously.

ψ

Amos walked awhile on the big desert island before he reached the village of the wretched souls. A hot sun scorched the earth and everyone was seated in the shade of their huts. Their bodies were totally dried and burned. These poor people were just skin and bones. With difficulty, a man got up and came to meet Amos.

"Go away," he said feebly. "We . . . we are doomed and—"

"I know of your fate," Amos interrupted him. "Your god is making fun of you and there seems to be no solution to your misfortune. Yet there is a way to get you out of this misery. I know how to make rain fall with two jars of water."

"We must not . . . drink the water we have," the man went on, swallowing the dust between his teeth with difficulty. "If we use the water the wrong way, our fate will be . . . forever sealed in suffering."

"Trust me. I think I can get you out of this fix. Bring me the first jar of water, as well as a large bucket, please," Amos said. "I also need some soap."

The mask wearer poured the contents of the first jar into the bucket. Then he removed his pants, soaked them in the water, and, using the soap, began to wash them. The villagers looked on in tears, feeling ever more hopeless. His washing done, Amos emptied the bucket and requested the second jar.

"But . . . but why did you do that?" the village chief begged him. "We are now condemned for eternity!"

"Trust me. I need the second jar, it is essential."

Believing everything was lost to them, anyway, the villagers agreed to his request. Amos took the second jar, emptied it into the bucket, and conscientiously rinsed his pants. When all trace of soap was gone, he dumped the water on the ground.

Then, to the despair of all, Amos asked, "May I dry my pants on this line?"

Discouraged, the village chief nodded. As soon as the pants were on the line, clouds covered the sun and a violent storm broke out. Amos smiled at the flabbergasted faces of the island inhabitants.

"My mother always told me that all it takes to make it

rain is to spread laundry on the line," he said. "The rain will come and spoil your work! Your god's puzzle is now solved. You are free to leave this island. The curse is no more. Take advantage of the rain. A boat is waiting for you at the dock. And do not forget to take a coin to pay your fare. The captain does not have an easy temper."

# —7—

## THE PURIFIER RETURNS

Beorf followed the trail of the fugitive cook, who rode his horse till morning and then stopped in a clearing not far from the limits of the Berrion kingdom. Beorf saw a man come to meet the cook. He was tall and strong and wore sturdy and shiny armor. He rode a big red horse. His shield was decorated with a coat of arms bearing huge snake heads. When the man removed his helmet, Beorf recognized him. It was Yaune the Purifier, former lord of Bratel-la-Grande. A long scar slashed his face, and he still had the word "murderer" tattooed across his forehead. He seemed even crueler and more vicious than in the past. He had accused Beorf's parents of sorcery and ordered that they be burned alive.

In his bear form, Beorf walked silently on all fours and got as close as possible to the two men. Hiding behind the trees at the edge of the forest that surrounded the clearing, the humanimal heard the cook say:

"Junos will leave the city of Berrion soon. He is to go to a desert of some kind. The body of the mask wearer will travel with them. I don't quite understand what happened to him. The lord will travel with strong warriors and a young girl from another land. Be wary of her, her powers are huge. Somehow she knew I was up to no good."

"Did someone follow you?" Yaune asked between clenched teeth.

"No, of course not!" the snitch said as he looked around nervously.

"Here are the thirty gold coins," Yaune said, throwing a little leather pouch at the man's face.

"Sorry, master, but we agreed on fifty gold coins as a reward!" the angry cook answered.

With no warning, Yaune drew his sword from its sheath and, in one stroke, cut the throat of his spy. The cook's body fell heavily to the ground. With the tip of his sword, Yaune picked up the small pouch.

"This is how you save money!" he whispered as he resheathed his sword.

Yaune took a good look around, put his helmet back on, and left in a gallop toward the forest. Once he had disappeared, Beorf emerged from the cover of the trees.

*I must go back to Berrion to warn Junos!* the humanimal told himself.

Careful to keep hidden, the young bear set off. Eventually he took to the road, where he was startled to see Yaune the Purifier in front of him. The disgraced knight removed his helmet.

"Bears are seldom taken by surprise, Beorf Bromanson!" Yaune said, pleased with himself. "You are much too plump to hide in the forest. Didn't your parents teach you that? Maybe not, since they died so young!"

Beorf regained his human form but kept his long claws and his powerful bear teeth. With these weapons, he had little to fear.

"Oh! You scare me!" Yaune said mockingly. "And since our last encounter in Bratel-la-Grande, I've been missing your friend Amos Daragon. What is he up to? And what is going on in Berrion?"

"You won't get anything out of me!" Beorf answered in a growl. "Never!"

"Very well, then I will have to kill you," Yaune said, drawing his sword.

Beorf followed his instincts. He took a powerful leap and landed on Yaune. He bit the knight's neck, directly under the right ear. Thrown from his horse, Yaune carried the humanimal down to the ground with him. Both fighters rapidly jumped to their feet.

"I had forgotten that man-beasts are full of surprises!" Yaune said, waving his huge sword with both hands. "Did you know that it took twelve of my Knights of Light just to immobilize your father? Quite a brute he was! Your mother, too, was difficult to catch, but we tricked her. I told her that you had been taken hostage and that if she did not cooperate, I was going to cut your throat! She followed us without any resistance and . . . we burned her alive. Your mother was stupid and sentimental, young man!"

Enraged, Beorf jumped on Yaune again. This time Yaune welcomed him with a powerful blow of his sword; Boerf fell to the ground in terrible pain.

"Poor Beorf!" Yaune sniggered. "What a pity! The last Bromanson family member is about to die."

Yaune kicked his adversary directly in his wound and, with his sword, cut deeply into Beorf's thigh. Ignoring his pain, Beorf got up swiftly and tore the knight's metal armor with one blow of his paw. The man went down but he, too, got up right away.

"If I had an army of humanimals like you, I would conquer the world in no time!" he said, looking at Beorf, who was bleeding profusely. "What strength for someone still young! Look what you did to my armor! Impressive! Too bad I have to kill you."

"Come on!" Beorf shouted. "We shall see which one of us emerges from this fight alive! I'm not scared of rats like you!"

He had hardly finished his sentence when he received a punch in the face that fractured his nose, but he managed to dodge a blow from his adversary's sword. Unfortunately,

Yaune's knee caught him in the stomach and cut his breathing short. He tried to bite Yaune's arm but failed. An avalanche of punches and blows fell over him. In spite of the knight's strength, Beorf held his own and remained standing. His face bloodied, his body broken by Yaune's attacks, Boerf finally found support against a tree trunk. His head was spinning and the pain was slowly paralyzing him.

"Farewell, you stupid man-bear!" he heard Yaune say.

He saw Yaune come at him with his sword, but could not move. Yaune's sword went through his body.

"This weapon poisons those it touches," Yaune sneered. "You will certainly die of your wounds."

In a desperate effort, Beorf leaped at Yaune's face and, with his claws, punctured one of his enemy's eyes. The knight shrieked in pain, but not before planting his sword into Beorf's body yet again.

"Are you going to die or not, you awful beast?" Yaune shouted. "Are you going to die once and for all?"

Yaune staggered back to his horse. His wounded eye bled abundantly. He rode off, leaving Beorf half dead on the ground. The poisoned sword had twice pierced his body. The young humanimal closed his eyes.

"I am going to see my parents again soon," he said calmly, smiling to himself.

Lord Junos had sent his men to search all of Berrion's nooks and crannies. They came back empty-handed. Beorf had disappeared and no one knew where he was. The knights had gone through the entire castle thoroughly, without neglecting the secret chambers and the attics; they had even gone to the cemetery—all in vain! There was no trace, no trail, no message.

Amid all this commotion, Lolya had requested that Amos's body be prepared as soon as possible. Junos chose twenty of his best knights for the journey. Counting the twenty Dogons, a delegation of forty men was to take the road to the pyramid of the Mahikui desert. Junos, his heart filled with apprehension, decided to leave without Beorf. The lord left his beloved city, hoping that Urban and Frilla would soon find the young humanimal.

Amos's body had been placed in a cart especially fitted for the occasion. Wrapped in several finely embroidered shrouds, he was laid out in a hammock that would protect him from the jerks of the cart over the road. A tent covered the cart so the sun would not burn Amos's corpse. Four beautiful horses pulled the cart. Heading the group, Junos gave the orders and the procession took off for a long two-month journey.

The first day of travel went smoothly. Come nightfall, though, right at the edge of the road where he had planned to set up camp, the lord of Berrion discovered a body lying on the ground. Lolya saw it too and gestured to her men.

They quickly brought back Beorf's swollen and bruised body. Junos rushed toward the young humanimal.

"Quick!" he shouted, seeing that Beorf's heart was still beating. "He is alive! We have to nurse him! Take him to Berrion! He does not have much time left. His heart is very weak!"

Lolya approached Beorf and put the palm of her hand over his forehead.

"His soul is clinging to life. He does not want to die," she said. "Beorf is fighting with all his might, but he will not survive the trip to Berrion. Trust me, Junos, I know how to bring him out of the realm of darkness."

Junos ordered that a tent be set up to receive Beorf and Lolya. The young queen went to work immediately, requesting a dozen leeches. She had noticed that Beorf's wounds were poisoned. His blood was not clotting. Five Dogons ran to the woods to fulfill her request. She also asked for black candles, the urine of a pregnant mare, and a hen. A few knights took off for the neighboring village.

"I know you can hear me," Lolya whispered as she bent toward Beorf. "You have to live, Beorf. Breathe fully. Your heart is beating regularly and your time has not come yet. Death is not asking for you. Trust me. I will get you out of this."

Lolya kept encouraging Beorf until the Dogons and the knights returned. Once she had all she needed at hand, she began putting the leeches over Beorf's body. Then she lit the candles and started a strange ritual. With the hen by her side, the young girl began to dance around Beorf's body while invoking a guédé—a greedy and dangerous spirit that constantly tried to extract the souls of the living from their human form. Guédés were responsible for deadly accidents, dangerous encounters, and the unhappy hazards of life. They drew their strength from the energy generated by the separation of the spirit and the body. In front of Lolya, above Beorf's body, a guédé appeared. An ugly face, pale and sickly, took shape in a transparent yellow cloud.

"What do you want of me?" the spirit asked.

"I demand that you give me back the soul of this boy," Lolya said firmly.

"I do not take orders from you, witch!" the guédé answered. "This soul is fighting beautifully, but I want to win the battle! I take huge pleasure in it. I draw a fantastic vital energy from it!"

"For the last time, guédé," Lolya threatened, "give him back to me and you will be free to leave in peace."

"One does not give orders to a guédé!" the transparent face shouted. "What could you do against me?"

"I know the ways of ancient peoples, the magic of the first kings of the earth," Lolya said proudly.

"You are lying!"

"Try me."

Lolya came close to the guédé, said a few words in an

archaic language, took hold of the spirit, and pushed it into the hen's body in one stroke. Prisoner of the bird, the spirit started to run in all directions. The hen, totally panicked, left the tent as the young queen laughed with satisfaction.

"That will teach you to argue with my commands!" Lolya shouted. "Go! Run fast! We will eat chicken tonight, stupid guédé! We will cook you, happily!"

Turning toward Beorf, she continued her incantations.

"Now I no longer fear for your spirit," she went on. "Let's take care of your wounds, and your survival is a sure thing. As long as I am close to you, no guédé will dare to interfere with me. They are stupid and fearful! Now, let me explain to you, Beorf. I know that you can hear me, and it is important that you fully understand the stages of your recovery. You are seriously poisoned. The leeches will gradually suck up the poison. Then they will fall off by themselves. As soon as you open your eyes, I will make you drink the mare's urine. You will see, it does not taste good, but it works very well. In fear that I might serve you some more, you will get better in no time!"

Junos came into the tent. "How is he?"

"He is out of danger," Lolya answered.

"Good!" The lord of Berrion sighed. "We just discovered the body of one of my cooks. The poor fellow has been beheaded. Strangely enough, he is the man you chased with a knife in the castle kitchen. The one you accused of treason. Lolya, tell me, do you know something I don't?"

"I know many things you don't," Lolya answered with a smile.

"Do you know who wounded Beorf and killed this cook?" Junos asked, worried.

"Look for a snake," Lolya answered. "A huge, angry snake!"

# —8—

## THE REALM OF OMAIN

Charon appeared suddenly on the deck of the boat.

"Get ready to cling together, my lovely passengers," he shouted. "We are arriving in the land of Omain!"

Amos ran starboard to look over the rail. His heart was beating madly. Omain was his birthplace and he had grown up there, learning the secrets of the forest. It was also where he had met Crivannia, the mermaid. A flood of memories overtook him. He saw the small cottage his father had built, his mother's tiny garden, and his long walks in the woods. Images of the river, of the fishing port, and of the surrounding mountains filled his mind. The ever-present smell of the sea came to him too.

The gangway fell and Amos saw a large crowd on the dock. The cemetery was filled with souls waiting patiently to come aboard. Amos wondered what kind of dreadful event could have sent so many of the peaceful people of Omain to their deaths. Every inhabitant of the kingdom was here! They were *all* dead! A huge catastrophe had probably killed them all at the same time. On the wharf, the ghosts showed deep cuts in their chests, their arms, and their legs. No one had survived this disaster. Many women and children were waiting for the boat. The sight was heartbreaking. Jerik appeared by his side.

"It is a war. You see, Master Daragon . . . here and there . . . the wounds of these people," he said. "They were . . . how do I say . . . killed with a sword. Someone . . . or . . . I mean something . . . an army, with ill intentions came here!"

Edonf, lord and master of the realm of Omain, was the first to board. He had not changed a bit. He was still portly, with three rolls of fat under his chin, and his face still resembled that of a huge sea toad, with protruding eyes that made him hideously ugly. He recognized Amos right away.

"Glad to see that you're dead too!" the fat lord cried dramatically. "It's about time this boat arrived. We've been waiting for days. We rang and rang the bell! It's impossible to get out of this miserable cemetery! By the way, young rascal, your donkey never gave me any gold. I thought of several ways to take revenge on you . . . but nothing is really important anymore."

"Could you tell me what happened?" Amos asked his former lord politely.

"A huge calamity fell on Omain," Edonf answered. "In fact, no one understands how or why it happened. The effect of surprise was the problem! There was nothing we could do. We were all dead in less than an hour!"

"I don't understand," Amos said. "Did a natural disaster take you by surprise?"

"Worse!" Edonf answered gravely. "We're dealing with a demon! He came to the village on a moonless night. He was tall and scarred and brandished a huge sword. Without any warning, he butchered the entire population! Going from house to house, he massacred everyone! From weak elderly to defenseless children, no one was spared. Then he came to the castle, my small fortress. In no time, he dispatched my personal guard. None of my soldiers managed to hold ground more than three seconds. A real demon, I tell you! In fact, he had the word 'murderer' tattooed on his forehead. Only a demon could be so strong."

Amos frowned. The pieces of the puzzle were slowly coming together for him. From Edonf's description Amos knew that Yaune the Purifier, former lord of the Knights of Light of Bratel-la-Grande, was the demon.

"What happened next?" Amos asked, anxious to know the whole story.

"This devil pulled me out of bed," Edonf went on. "He told me that he was going to take possession of my realm for many years. The next thing I knew, his sword pierced my body and my soul arrived in this cemetery. Well, that's what happened to everybody except for one man. Look over there—he's coming on board now. Nobody knows him. He appeared in Omain a few days ago. He doesn't say a word, just keeps quiet in his corner. From what I saw, his throat was cut."

Amos approached the man and recognized him as one of the cooks from Berrion.

"What happened to you?" Amos asked him.

"You're here? Then you're truly dead?" said the astonished cook. "The queen of the Dogons really killed you?"

Not willing to explain the reasons for his presence on the boat, Amos answered affirmatively.

"Now that I'm dead, I might as well tell you everything," the cook said, eager to confess. "In addition to being a cook for the past few weeks, I was also working as a spy for a knight whose coat of arms had snake heads. He never told me his name, but at the time, I admired him. Now I have a different opinion. Anyway, he promised me fifty gold coins to provide him with vital information. He had an old insult to avenge. He wanted to know what was going on in Berrion. One evening, I learned that your body had been exhumed and that it was to be taken to a faraway desert—"

"Wait," Amos interrupted him. "You say my body was exhumed? That it was taken out of the cemetery?"

"Yes, the queen of the Dogons ordered it. Some spirit possessed her, something called a baron or the like, I don't remember. Her voice became very deep and she threatened everybody, demanding that your body be brought to the desert of . . . of . . . I can't remember that either."

"Did she say why my body had to be taken away?" Amos pressed, more and more interested.

"She said that you were not really dead! It's difficult to understand. I don't know anything more, except that the mask she gave you was in fact a gift from this baron. It was meant to gain your confidence."

Uriel, who was standing near Amos, paid close attention to the conversation. He cleared his throat.

"They are taking your body to the Mahikui desert," the learned man said.

"But why?" Amos asked. "And how do you know this, Uriel?"

"To answer your second question, I studied many legends and old tales in order to understand the mentality of different peoples. Now, why take your body to the Mahikui desert? It's simple! We are sailing toward Braha, the City of the Dead. Actually, this city existed for a long time in the real world. A magnificent city! An incomparable jewel! Then, *poof*! It was totally buried under the sands of the Mahikui desert during a violent storm. Later, the gods chose this place to receive the souls of the dead for judgment. They built two doors: one that led to the astral world of the positive gods, and the other that opened directly to the negative plans of the gods of evil and chaos. A small part of this city exists at the same time in the world of the dead and the world of the living. It is, it seems, the only place of its kind. It is said that at the top of the great pyramid of the city center there is a ceremonial room that is the junction between the two universes. Through this room, it is possible to go from one world to the other. The living who march in the desert are able to see the top of this pyramid, which sticks out of the sands, and to enter through a secret door. But for the dead who arrive in Braha, the top of this pyramid is invisible because clouds cover it."

"I see," Amos said pensively. "So the ceremonial room at the top of the pyramid is where the dead can access the world of the living, and vice versa?"

Uriel nodded.

"But how? What magic could make it possible?"

"I don't know. I never found the answer," Uriel replied, a little embarrassed. "With time, the knowledge got lost. It is what we call a mystery of the gods, a powerful magic inaccessible to men."

Jerik moved closer to them. Irritated by their discussion, he absentmindedly tried to put his head back on his shoulders, but it fell backward and almost plunged overboard.

"This is what I was trying to explain to you!" he shouted as he caught his head. "From the moment you and I first talked . . . do you remember, Master Daragon? The first time, I wanted to tell you . . . I mean . . . all this?"

"All right. But I still don't understand your story about the key," Amos answered.

"Well ... our learned companion can better explain ... ," Jerik said, pleased with Uriel's performance so far.

Uriel nodded. "From what I know, and from snatches of your conversations," he began, "I believe I can shed some light on your mission in Braha. I mentioned two doors."

"I remember," Amos confirmed.

"Well, these doors are now closed, and the three magistrates are faced with a huge problem. The city is overcrowded with souls who arrive by boat every day, and there is no exit through which they can leave. Is that right, Jerik?"

"Yes, so simple to explain this way ... I mean ... perfect ... exactly ... right on the nose!" answered Mertellus's secretary.

"Let's continue," Uriel said. "Amos, you must help by opening the doors in question. The gods probably closed them for an unknown reason. But there is a key. The legend says that the first magistrate of Braha had it made by an elf, without the gods' knowledge. Just as in your case, young Master Daragon, the elf's soul was removed from her body with the promise that her death would be temporary. But even after she finished her work, the locksmith was not permitted to return to the world of the living. She had been deceived! Angry at having been fooled and unable to resume her life, the elf hid the key in the depths of the city— and bewitched it in such manner that no living being can get to it. She then put two dangerous guards in charge of protecting it and disappeared without telling her secret to anyone. This is what the legend says, but . . . since I know the legend, it is clear that this elf must have confided in someone. Otherwise, I would never have heard her story!"

"There we are . . . at last . . . a fine explanation!" Jerik shouted, impressed by Uriel's lies.

"But," Amos said pensively, "nothing is more uncertain than this story. A legend is just a legend."

"That is true . . . but these tales are usually clues that cannot be neglected," Uriel answered.

Amos nodded and walked a ways off to think.

"I lie with facility and I can murder just as easily!" Uriel whispered to Jerik.

"No . . . I think . . . we are manipulating him without any problem. With what you just said . . . he will do exactly what we . . . well . . . what Seth expects of him."

"I rather like this boy. Too bad I have to eliminate him!" Uriel said.

ψ

Amos was deep in thought as he watched the landscape go by. If Lolya had had his body brought to the pyramid, she surely had good reason to take such a risk.

*According to the legend of the elf locksmith,* Amos thought, *the key can only be taken by a living being, but . . . there is only one way to enter into the city of Braha—as a ghost. At the right moment, I shall probably reintegrate my body to be able to put my hand on the key. That is why Lolya had my body brought to the pyramid! I am here as a ghost to find the hiding place of the key. That is what is expected of me. Yet something isn't right. The gods didn't just lock the doors to heaven and to hell without good reason . . . so I have to find out what's really behind all this!*

Filled with passengers, the boat left the wharf of Omain's cemetery. On board were all the inhabitants of the island of the damned and all those of Edonf's realm, in addition to those who had boarded here and there from the many cemeteries that bordered the river. From the hold to the upper deck, there were ghosts everywhere!

"We're full! No more ports of call!" Charon announced from the deck. "Try to make yourselves comfortable. In three weeks, we will arrive in Braha."

"Three weeks!" Amos sighed. "Next time, I'll try to reserve a cabin."

# —9—

## SETH'S SCHEME

"So, Seth, where is this army that you promised me?" Yaune the Purifier asked bluntly.

Seated on a gold throne in a temple built entirely of human bones, Seth, the god of jealousy and treachery, smiled viciously. He swung his head up and down as a sign of assent. He was frightening to behold, with light red skin and hands that looked like powerful eagle's talons.

"Little knight of my heart, don't you have any confidence in me?" he asked.

"It seems you know how to read souls!" Yaune answered with contempt. "I have no confidence in you, no respect for you, and not even an ounce of affection for you, you ugly venomous snake!"

Seth let out a deep, repulsive chuckle.

"Hatred," he said, "is such a strong feeling! You are teaching me a lot about humanity, pitiful knight. Serve me well and you will be rewarded accordingly!"

"With you, Seth, I serve my own interest first. Give me what you promised me!"

"And you dare to give orders!" Seth laughed even harder. "First, tell me what happened to your eye! Did a mosquito bite you?"

"You know very well what happened!" Yaune answered, enraged. "It was the humanimal, the young Bromanson. I underestimated his last burst of energy before his death. That happens when you're just a simple mortal. But of course, you wouldn't know what I'm talking about. Gods are infallible! Particularly when it comes to destroying a twelve-year-old mask wearer!"

"Do not mock me, Yaune!" the god said, slowly articulating each of his words. "My patience is not limitless! If I failed in Bratel-la-Grande, it is because of that stupid sorcerer, Karmakas. Amos Daragon was lucky, that is all, and—"

"It doesn't matter!" The knight cut him short. "Because of Amos Daragon, I lost my kingdom and my lands. I also lost the Knights of Light, who now take their orders from Barthelemy. I am fed up! After being banished from Bratel-la-Grande with this horrid tattoo on my forehead, after weeks of misery and wandering, I met you and you promised me—"

"Quiet!" Seth shouted.

The god's voice was so strong that it threw Yaune against the wall at the other end of the temple. The knight fell loudly to the ground. He raised his head with difficulty. His gaze met that of Seth's, who had risen from his throne.

"During our first encounter, I asked you to conquer the realm of Omain and I offered you a sword with a poisoned blade. I admit that you have performed well. Alone, you managed to eliminate all trace of human life in that region. You razed the kingdom in a vicious and immoral way. You slaughtered children, brutally killed grandmothers, and even drank Edonf's blood while it was still warm! You are thirsty for revenge, and I am about to reward your devotion to me. I always keep my word with those who serve me well. Today, Yaune, is the day you receive your first promotion!"

The god returned to his throne and sat comfortably. After a moment of silence, Seth motioned the knight to come closer.

"You will soon have an army . . . a magnificent army! Amos Daragon is at this moment working unknowingly to offer you this army on a silver platter. You seem skeptical. Listen carefully and note that Seth, god of jealousy and treachery, is also a skillful strategist."

Yaune approached and answered respectfully this time. "I never doubted you or your intelligence, great Seth!"

"You lie so easily, Yaune! That's what I like best about you!"

"Speak, I am all ears."

"Not that long ago," Seth began, "I kidnapped the supreme god of justice, Forseti, with the help of some divine friends. His disappearance had unfortunate consequences, one of them being the locking of the doors out of Braha. I already mentioned the City of the Dead to you."

"Yes," Yaune answered. "The great city of the last judgment, buried in the Mahikui desert, which can be reached only by the Styx. I remember. Go on!"

"In this city, three judges decide the fate of the ghosts waiting for their judgment. The judges are impartial and answer to Forseti in person. But sometimes the rot that inhabits the world of the living contaminates that of the dead. In other words, it is possible to bribe a judge. Ganhaus, one of the judges, works for me. In exchange, I promised to liberate his elder brother's soul from the depths of hell. His brother's name is Uriel, and he was a notorious murderer."

"And how is this going to give me a magnificent army?" Yaune asked feverishly.

"Listen, imbecile! I'm getting there!" Seth answered, annoyed and threatening. "Savor my words and enjoy my treachery! Together we will devise a perfect scheme—a pure jewel of malice. With Forseti now my prisoner, the doors of hell and heaven are shut. The three judges have been trying to find a solution to the overcrowding in Braha. Ganhaus very cleverly invented an incredible tale about gypsies that confirmed the existence of the key of Braha. Made by an elf locksmith and kept in the depths of the city, this key is supposed to be the only way to open the doors. But who would be able to find the key other than a human courageous enough to undertake such a foolish mission?"

"Amos Daragon!" Yaune said, laughing.

"Exactly! He's the one we need. Jerik Svenkhamr, a stupid petty thief who is Mertellus's secretary and who also works for me, mentioned the young mask wearer. Everyone fell for it! Mertellus immediately got in touch with Baron Samedi, a lower-caste god who works in the administration services of the dead and the management of souls, to have him make arrangements for Amos to come to Braha. Then, as promised, I liberated Uriel from hell and had him board Charon's boat, right after Amos. He's pretending to be a respectable learned scientist and a literary man—just as I devised. The very opposite of his true self! His mission is to tell Amos the false story of the elf and to get rid of him when the time comes."

"But wait," Yaune said.

Seth held up a hand and continued. "The key of Braha *does* exist. But it is only meant to open the passage at the top of the pyramid, not the doors of the positive and negative worlds. It is used to open an ethereal pathway between Braha and the world of the living. Believe me, faithful servant, you will soon be the leader of a huge army of ghosts. At this very moment, our envoys are recruiting the best of them. As the leader of this forceful army, you will be invincible! You will have your revenge over Junos, Barthelemy, and all those who loathe you so much. Then, together, we will conquer Earth and destroy the equilibrium of the living."

Satisfied, Yaune burst out laughing. "Finally the time for revenge has come," he said with glee. "What's more, it is the young mask wearer who will give me the means to retaliate. I cannot believe it. You are a genius, Seth! A question, though: How will Amos manage to find the key?"

"Let's just say some friends of mine are putting pressure on Forseti to make sure he reveals where the key is hidden," Seth confided. "As soon as I know where it is, I will inform Jerik, who will direct Amos in his quest. As in the invented story of the elf locksmith, two guards watch over the key and only a living human can take it. Two small problems that the mask wearer will surely solve for us! He is a clever boy! Only one thing bothers me."

"What is it?" Yaune asked, worried.

"Lolya," the god answered pensively. "I know that she is the envoy of Baron Samedi and that she is working toward our success in spite of herself, but she is hiding something. A terrible force grows in her day after day. As much as I try to clear this mystery, I do not see what it is. I do not trust her. Hire a mercenary army and kill Lolya.

Do not underestimate her, because my inability to understand her comes under godly magic. Then you will take Amos Daragon's body to the pyramid of the Mahikui desert yourself."

"I will carry out your wishes," Yaune said, bowing his head.

"Come closer," Seth ordered him.

Yaune took a few steps toward Seth. With one hand, the god grabbed him by the throat and raised him off the ground. Laughing heartily, the snake god pulled an eye from his own head and put it in the knight's open socket. The fusion between the god's eyeball and Yaune's body filled the knight with a dreadful pain. It was like being branded. Seth let go and Yaune tumbled to the ground in a fit of spasms. The god's eye was now a part of him.

"That is my gift! An eye to replace the one you lost," Seth declared. "This reptile eye suits you well! You will be able to see in the dark, and from now on, no move by your enemy will escape you. Through this eye, I will also be able to see what you see and follow your every move. In other words, I will accompany you wherever you go! I trusted Karmakas too much in Bratel-la-Grande; I am not about to make the same mistake again. You may go now!"

The temple of bones gradually disappeared. Yaune remained on the grass in the forest. His new eye hurt terribly. Jogging along, the knight went to his residence, the former fortified castle of Lord Edonf. When he arrived, his eyes met his reflection in a mirror. It was a shock! The eye that Seth had given him had a dark yellow iris and the elongated pupil of a cat. Perfectly round, it was one and a half times larger than a normal eye. It deformed his face. Blood was still running down his cheek. Unable to accept his new face, Yaune smashed the mirror.

"When the time comes, I will take my revenge on you, Seth!" he shouted.

# —10—

## BRAHA, CITY OF THE DEAD

J erik was the first to see the great city of Braha. It appeared through a thick and gray morning fog. The secretary was quick to wake Amos and Uriel.

"Come . . . hurry . . . ," he shouted. "You will see something very beautiful . . . I mean . . . rather . . . magnificent . . . no . . . imposing!"

The two travelers had trouble opening their eyes. Stepping over the ghosts sleeping on the deck, they followed Jerik to the front of the boat. One of the two skeletons of Charon's crew perched on the broken figurehead, waiting to see the sight too. He smoked his pipe quietly. Since he had no lungs, the smoke he inhaled escaped through the open space between his ribs. The fog that surrounded the boat dissipated gradually, yet the cloud ceiling remained very low.

Amos glimpsed the city of Braha, still far away. He was dazzled by its magnificence. As the boat approached, the city took on a soft reddish color. Although it was early morning, the mask wearer had the impression that he was watching the sun set. In the city center, one could see rays of orange and yellow light hit the thick layer of clouds, coloring them with thousands of lights. In the sky, no sun, no moon, not even a star! The light was coming from the city.

As they went closer, Amos watched scores of splendid transparent angels fly above the silvery slate roofs. The winged beings played their trumpets to greet the newcomers. The mask wearer could not believe his eyes. Breathless in front of such beauty, he also saw dozens of demons posted on both sides of the river. They were banging on large drums from which smoke and flames came out. In the sky, the angels' music took shape and formed blue curved lines spotted with golden light. The beauty of the spectacle was impressive.

Braha was immense. Its size and splendor defied imagination. Built on the sides of two steep mountains, it opened toward the sky like a large V. The Styx ran at the bottom of the city, directly at its center. There were thousands of houses rising on several levels; there were also grand castles and sumptuous temples. Every cult, every belief, and all the godly figures of every nation were gathered there. The temples, competing with each other in beauty, had been built with care out of the finest materials. Gold and silver, diamonds and crystals, rare marble and precious stones decorated every building. Fine ornamentations cut out of exotic wood by master craftsmen had been used to enhance the trimmings of the huge church towers.

Openmouthed, Amos looked on in silence at the opulence before him. The passengers, now awake and filled with admiration, were also speechless. All the city's statues, whether ornamental gargoyles or heroes immortalized in stone, walked freely. They politely greeted each other and sometimes stopped to chat. The streets were crowded with luminous specters that, in a constant back-and-forth, attended to their business. Lots of farmers' markets welcomed the ghostly clients. They offered rotten tomatoes and wilted salads. Clouds of black flies gathered over putrefying pieces of meat.

Hundreds of fires used to make offerings to the gods burned here and there, illuminating the city. In the windows of each house, dozens of candles were lit, giving Braha a fairy-tale-like atmosphere. Skeletons, armed with swords and shields, were posted at almost every street corner. When Amos asked what their role was, Jerik said that they were in charge of city security.

The wealthiest specters rode in carts drawn by horse skeletons. Some sinister-looking specters were begging in the streets. Raising his eyes, Amos saw nearly twenty winged horses ridden by strong women in armor. They darted across the sky at an amazing speed while shouting war cries and howling songs in a language that made him think of thunderclaps.

"According to my studies," Uriel explained, "these women are Valkyries. Men from the north, called Vikings, never take Charon's boat to come here. The Valkyries take care of the transportation of these valorous warriors who died in combat."

"The god Odin grants them this special treatment!" Charon shouted. He had entrusted the helm to the skeleton second mate and had come near the boat's prow. "I lose a great deal of money because of this. These crazy ladies are always racing around and bothering everybody."

As it neared the port, the boat passed under imposing bridges. The masts of Charon's boat knocked their stone structures, which dematerialized slightly to let it go by without damage.

On the shores of the Styx, Amos saw dozens of terraces, beautiful restaurants, and street entertainers. Men and women of all races, humans as well as elves, minotaurs and gorgons, devils and angels, centaurs and sprites, strolled around in their ghostly vaporous shapes. Their colors varied from snow-white to coal-black. Leather suits, precious silks, and gold jewels mingled with dirty and rusty armor. Scarred humans mixed with a crowd of repulsive beings of an indescribable ugliness.

Looking to the highest level of the town, Amos was able to see the base of the great pyramid mentioned in the legends Uriel had told him. The top disappeared into the clouds. Each of the pyramid's stones was the size of a whale.

Charon came to rest on the rail by Amos's side.

"Welcome to Braha, young mask wearer," he said softly. "Here, people live exactly as they did before their deaths. All who believed in a god still believe; those who had a conscience, however tiny, find themselves in Braha pending the last judgment. Those who were tightfisted, like me, remain tightfisted here. The spiritual guides as well as the healers, the murderers as well as the magicians, they are all here! They are just as bad or as good as they were during their lives. In this city, you do not change, you do not get better, you just wait patiently, that is all! You wait to meet Judge Mertellus and his colleagues to find out your fate. Be very careful! In this city you will find the better and the worse. No one can kill you, but many can make you suffer. Everything is amplified here, larger than in real life. That's my warning. Thanks again for liberating the people on the island of the damned. I owe you. One day I will pay you back if I can!"

Charon turned toward the crowd of specters swarming the boat.

"Get ready to go ashore, you good-for-nothing bums!" he shouted. "We are going to dock! I hope you enjoyed your trip! I, for one, hated it!"

The boat docked and all the passengers rushed toward the gangway. Mertellus, Ganhaus, and Korrillion were waiting on the wharf. When they saw Jerik waving to them, his smiling head under his arm, the judges relaxed.

"I think he managed to bring the mask wearer," Ganhaus said to Mertellus.

"I'll believe it only when the mask wearer is right in front of me," the first magistrate answered nervously.

"Look! They're coming down! They're coming down!" Korrillion repeated. "It must be the man with the finely shaped beard."

The three magistrates ran to Uriel to welcome him warmly. Two of them had mistaken the man for someone else. But none of them could have imagined that the real mask wearer was in fact a mere twelve-year-old boy. They heaped compliments and warm welcomes upon Uriel. Of course, Ganhaus had recognized his brother. But he grudgingly played along as the scholar tried unsuccessfully to get a word in.

As Amos wondered how to stop the three eager and talkative men, he had an idea. He winked at Uriel! The scholar understood that Amos wanted him to keep pretending to be the mask wearer. Jerik was about to tell the truth, but Amos crushed his toes to cut him short.

"It is better this way," Amos told the secretary. "It buys me extra time."

Amos came forward and coughed three times to catch the three magistrates' attention. The judges turned and looked at him. In turn Amos looked at Uriel.

"Yes, let me introduce my young pupil—I mean, my research assistant. His name is . . ."

"Darwich Socks," Amos said spontaneously.

The judges did not seem surprised. They had heard so

many strange and funny names. They smiled politely and paid no more attention to Amos.

"He is from the famous family of Socks of . . . the . . . Foot of the Smoking Mountain!" Uriel said. "Well, let us go back to our business!"

"Yes, follow us, we will take you to your apartments in the palace," Mertellus went on, happy with this meeting.

"The trip must have tired you out," Korrillion said. "But you will discover that ghosts generally do not need to sleep. It is only a reflex that lingers for some time after death. For now, though, we will not keep you from taking a little nap. We want you to be in the best shape in the shortest time!"

Uriel, the three judges, Amos, and Jerik took a cart driven by a skeleton. Drawn by the bones of four horses, the vehicle disappeared quickly within the milling crowd of specters.

"Mertellus did not even acknowledge you!" Amos said to Jerik. The two of them were seated at the top of the cart. "Is that normal?"

"You see . . . I mean . . . ," the secretary said, holding his head firmly between his hands. "How do I say it . . . I obey orders and . . . that's all!"

"Too bad," Amos answered. "They do not appreciate your worth."

"Thank you . . . uh . . . thanks a lot!" Jerik responded, visibly touched.

The palace was also something to behold. Octagonal

in shape, it was topped with a huge dome. A large staircase spiraled out of the roof and climbed directly toward the sky through the clouds. The building was ornate, with thousands of stone gargoyles that were flying freely, climbing the walls, playing dice, or chatting. As soon as Mertellus stepped out of the cart, all the gargoyles stopped moving. The flying ones fell to the ground or crashed against a wall. Others plunged into the great fountain right in front of the palace.

Amos watched the scene a little stunned, not understanding this change of attitude. The gargoyles, which had been restless a few seconds ago, were now frozen like statues. Amos was about to ask why the commotion had stopped, but Jerik spoke first.

"When the cat's away the mice will play! When the judge goes out . . . uh . . . the gargoyles take advantage of it. Mertellus does not like turmoil and . . . I mean . . . that the ornaments of his palace . . . are forbidden to move. He is the only one in this city who is so stern! A real tyrant when it comes . . . uh . . . to his statues' freedom . . . of expression!"

"He is not a very pleasant magistrate," Amos said.

"Do you know one . . . who is?" Jerik answered coldly.

They all entered the palace.

"Welcome to the hall of justice," Mertellus said solemnly. "This is where good and evil are judged, where eternity begins. The decisions made within these walls are always just, and we are proud of that. Jerik, take your friend to his room. I will look after our guest, the dear, the extraordinary Mr. Daragon."

Slightly panicked, Uriel looked at Amos as if to say, "And now what do I do?" The mask wearer smiled to reassure him and followed Jerik quickly. Amos was sure that Uriel would play his part perfectly. As he walked to his room, Amos admired the beauty of the palace. The walls were covered with finely woven tapestries, red velvet curtains, and stained-glass windows, and thick carpets blanketed the floor. There were numerous libraries, dens, offices, and conference rooms. Jerik pushed a door open.

"Here we are. It is small, but . . . it is better than sleeping outside. You know . . . Master Daragon . . . you should envy Uriel . . . who is going to sleep . . . in the apartment reserved for the gods' envoys . . . for important people! It is grand."

"It's much better for me this way," Amos said, smiling. "I know what my mission is and I do not need to be told again. Uriel is very learned and he has gracious manners. I could not wish for a better representative."

"And now . . . what do we do?" Jerik inquired.

"You stay here and I will take a walk around the city. I have something to find out!"

# —11—

## DARWICH SOCKS

The three judges had copious food and drink served to their guest; then Ganhaus offered to take the pretend mask wearer to his apartments.

"Why do you act as if you're Amos Daragon?" he was finally able to ask his brother. "And where is the real mask wearer hiding?"

"Happy to see you too," Uriel answered. "We haven't seen each other in years. You've changed a lot, young brother, and I am glad to see that you have become a very important person."

"Listen to me, Uriel, we do not have time to waste on small talk! I don't like you and I never did. I became a judge precisely to punish the kind of man you turned out to be. Murderers disgust me. If I had you freed from hell, it was for a specific reason."

"I can see that you have a deep sense of family!" Uriel snickered. "You always used Father, Mother, and me to achieve your ambitions. Even dead and buried, you haven't changed! You've become worse than me, your honor!"

"Listen to me carefully. I had you freed from the eternal torments and fire of hell and you owe me. You are here to do away with Amos Daragon, and to get hold of the key of Braha. Seth told you this himself, I believe."

"Yes, and that is all I know," Uriel confirmed. "I was also to tell Amos the story of an elf locksmith."

"But where is this famous Amos Daragon?"

Uriel, murderer that he was, answered with a wicked grin. "I introduced him to you under the name of Darwich Socks. He is the mask wearer!"

"I beg your pardon? The boy?"

"Not just any boy. I played along with his game so as not to un*mask*—ha!—myself too quickly. It is an excellent cover for him as well as for me."

"What is he like?"

"This boy's intelligence and quick mind are exceptional. And to think I pretended to be a man of learning in front of him! It was tough. Fortunately, during the long journey, his attention was entirely on his mission. We talked a lot and played cards. He's a very honest and respectful boy. He caught me cheating a few times and never mentioned it openly. But now, tell me, what do you expect me to do next?"

"I want you to follow Amos Daragon, and when he finds the key of Braha, steal it from him. Throw his body in the Styx! I want you to hand me the key, that is all!"

"But it is Seth who wants the key. I am supposed to give it to him, not you!"

"Listen, brother," Ganhaus answered, amused. "I have the power to send you back to hell! If you follow my orders I promise you will be pardoned and sent to paradise. If not, as soon as the doors reopen, I will make sure you return to the fire and the demons! I am a judge. Remember that. With a file such as yours, your case will be decided quickly! Think it over. I will come back for your answer."

"But why do you want this key?"

"That is none of your business!" Ganhaus answered. Then he mumbled, "I will soon be a god."

For the past few days, Amos had been strolling around Braha. He was looking for clues, for a trail to follow and carry his quest to success. Uriel, who still played the role of mask wearer, seemed perfectly at ease with the judges; Amos saw him often in Ganhaus's company. The scholar was reserved and not very talkative when Amos was around. He and Amos had had little contact since their arrival in Braha, but Amos was not concerned. Only one thing upset him: as he walked around the city, he always felt as if he was being followed. He constantly sensed a piercing gaze on his back, a disturbing presence that spied on his every move. For comfort, he told himself that walking in a town populated by ghosts was enough to make anyone paranoid.

Soon enough, Amos made some unexpected acquaintances. One day, at the corner of a very busy street, he came face to face with Vincenc, a seven-foot-tall skeleton who was begging for money. He was telling passersby his life story and asking for money to buy back his bones. Because he had been very tall when he was alive, a famous anatomy professor had offered him a deal: the giant would be paid ten gold coins if he promised to bequeath his skeleton to the professor so that he could study it after Vincenc's death. The contract was signed quickly: Vincenc was convinced that the old professor would die before him, and more than anything, he badly needed the money to pay off debts he had incurred in the many pubs of the area. Unfortunately, nothing happened as expected. Shortly after paying off his debts, the poor giant drowned in the river. His body was never found. His skeleton was now the property of the professor, while his soul remained prisoner in Braha. Vincenc was begging, hoping to gather the ten gold coins needed to buy his bones back. No one ever gave him enough money, so the poor skeleton kept telling his pathetic story.

Amos also met Angess. She sat next to him on a park bench and asked him if he had seen Peten, her great love. She was dressed in white, with a long sword piercing her neck. Her dress was stained with blood. When she had been alive, Angess had fallen in love with Peten and wanted to marry him. But her father had decided otherwise. He had chosen another man for her, someone more respectable and richer. Angess had to meet Peten in secret, and one day her father surprised them. Enraged, he raised his sword to strike Peten, but Angess threw herself between them to protect him. The sword pierced her neck. Since that day, the poor girl had been wandering through Braha, looking for Peten.

One morning, Amos ventured out to a totally deserted plaza located at the back of an imposing monastery. The place was magnificent, and Amos wondered why everyone seemed to avoid such a charming spot. In the center of the plaza sat a beautiful fountain bordered by huge oak trees. But the mask wearer soon understood why the place was empty: three massive dogs came out of nowhere and furiously tried to attack him. Amos barely escaped being torn to pieces. As soon as he left the plaza, the dogs disappeared.

Amos later learned that these dogs were actually three condemned criminals. In life they had robbed a monk's tomb. The criminals had dug up the holy man's grave because it supposedly contained valuable religious artifacts. As they were about to grab the sacred treasure, the dead monk had risen and damned them for eternity. The tomb looters had thus been transformed into massive black dogs; and ever since, they had been guarding the treasure to make sure the monk rested in peace.

Braha was filled with beings, each stranger than the

last. There was also a castle haunted by a werewolf, and an avenue where a crazy barber loved shaving the heads of the ghosts who passed by. In another part of town, on the hour, every hour, a newly married woman popped out of a well singing religious chants. Once she was done, she plunged back into the hole, screaming horribly. Amos saw pirates having fun trying to board a building as they would a ship. The city was in a constant state of chaos and wild energy. Amos relished discovering all its areas and inhabitants. His curiosity always made him meet fascinating spirits.

A new day was beginning for Amos. He had been walking in Braha for about an hour. So far, he had found no clue, no trail that could lead him to the key of Braha. He inquired everywhere, listened to the rumors circulating in the city, but no one seemed to know the famous legend. As he was strolling among the crowd of specters, Amos noticed that Jerik was following him. He continued to walk as if he had not seen the secretary. But why was Jerik spying on him? Was it to make sure he was safe? After all, Amos did not know the city; the secretary probably wanted to watch over him.

For fun, Amos decided to surprise his friend. He ran straight ahead and then quickly turned into a small, dark alley. Once there, he squatted, ready to jump out at Jerik when he passed. The secretary was going to have the fright of a lifetime! Suddenly Amos felt a presence behind him. He turned and saw a disturbing giant, as big as a whale, bald and scarred. With one hand, the giant grabbed Amos and dragged him farther into the dark alley.

A few seconds later, Amos was thrown on top of a trash pile.

"Admit that you are a thief!" the giant commanded. He was carrying a huge hammer in one hand. "You were trying to hide from the skeletons, those rotten skeletons that rule and watch and decide over everything. You were trying to flee from them. You are a thief, are you not? I know thieves. . . ."

Amos knew better than to contradict an excited giant who was ready to strike him.

"Yes," he said quickly. "My name is Darwich Socks. I am a thief, the best thief in the city, and I was fleeing the skeletons!"

"Good!" the big toothless warrior answered. "Good, very good! Come with me, I know some people who are having a party. I will introduce you to my boss. He, too, is a thief. I am sure that he will like you. Then you will be my servant. I always wanted to be served; it looks more serious to have a servant! Do you agree or do I get angry?"

"I accept with pleasure," Amos answered as he swallowed hard. "It will be a great honor to serve you, Master . . ."

"'Master'?" repeated the delighted giant. "That has

a nice sound to it! It will be Master Ougocil. That is my name, Ougocil!"

"Very well, where are we going?" Amos asked as he looked around to see how he could possibly slip away.

"I am not supposed to tell you," the big Ougocil answered. "It is a secret. The thieves' guild of Braha does not like its secrets revealed!"

"But how do we go there, then? If we walk together, I will surely see where the guild hides out."

"Not if you are asleep!" Ougocil answered, raising his weapon.

Ougocil knocked Amos on the head with his hammer. He lost consciousness. As Charon had told him on the boat, one could not die in Braha, but one could suffer a great deal. Amos remembered these words as he woke up. An awful headache was torturing him pitilessly.

When he opened his eyes, Amos looked around. His vision finally cleared and came back to normal. He was lying on the floor of a room draped in red velvet curtains. There were hundreds of specters dancing, drinking, and having fun. They were in a grand hall. All the guests were wearing white wigs, and clothes adorned with sumptuous embroidery. The soft music of a chamber orchestra imparted an uncommon lightness to the place.

When he tried to move from his uncomfortable position, Amos realized that his neck was chained to the foot of a thronelike chair. He raised his eyes and saw an elf seated on the chair who looked like a prince. He was white-haired and black-skinned and had pointed ears. His teeth were perfect, his face was exceptionally beautiful, and his movements had the gracefulness of an angel's. He looked at Amos, tied at his feet like a domesticated animal.

"Good evening, Darwich Socks! Ougocil, the stupidest of Braha's barbarians, brought you here," he said, smiling maliciously. "He wanted you to be his servant, but the idiot does not understand that one cannot *own* a servant when one *is* a servant. He is as dumb as can be. Ougocil is also the fiercest fighter I have ever seen. This is why he is my personal guard. He can face a whole army by himself. Unfortunately, his stupidity equals his courage. Yes, I am the master of this place and you are my prisoner. I am the leader of the guild of thieves. All the people you see here are first-class low-lifes, cutthroat bandits. There are murderers, pickpockets, poisoners, and traitors. None you can trust. We are all waiting for the last judgment, which will throw us in hell, but in the meantime we're having a grand time! We are hiding! We shun the skeletons' justice! In Braha, nothing changes. But, tell me, young man, you declare that you are the best thief in the city? Is that what you told this foolheaded oaf?"

Amos wasn't sure how to respond. He had lied to try to save his life, and now that lie might backfire. He quickly considered the situation. He was tied up like a dog, the prisoner of this wicked elf. There was nothing he could do to get out of this trap! So Amos decided to play along.

"Yes, I am indeed the best thief in this city!" he said, doing his best to sound confident.

"I knew you would say that," the elf answered. "All thieves are pretentious boasters! Well, we shall see whether that is true or not, my friend. We will put you to the test. I've devised a little game for my entertainment. One has time to kill.

"At the center of this room, there is a large table. Do you see it behind the people who are dancing?"

"Yes, I see it," Amos confirmed.

"Well, on that table there is a tray containing about a hundred golden teaspoons. Five guards watch over this tray very carefully. It holds my best cutlery, which I use for special occasions. You will steal one of the spoons and bring it to me! If you succeed, I will let you go. If you fail, I will throw you in the Styx, where your soul will dissolve. Do you understand? I do not like liars, and I like braggarts even less. Before you start, let me introduce you to Shadow."

A young boy, absolutely identical to Amos, approached them.

"He is surprising, you will see," the elf said. "Go, Shadow, fetch one of those golden spoons for me without being noticed."

Shadow disappeared in the crowd. In less than a second, he took on the appearance of a dancer, then of another one, then of a woman, and finally that of a child. Unnoticed, he slowly approached the table.

"Shadow is the greatest thief in the city!" the elf told Amos. "He is the last surviving member of his race in Braha. The people of the dark, as they were called, left the living world and that of the dead a long time ago. Look at how he changes his appearance and expressions. His body is made of vapor that solidifies to take the form he wants. He is amazing! He can shape-shift as easily into an object as a human."

Now close to the table, Shadow assumed the appearance of one of the guards. He sneezed to attract attention, changed shape once more, leaned over the table, pretended to faint, and rapidly grabbed a spoon. He slipped it into his sleeve and dashed to the dance floor. Twenty seconds later, looking like a very beautiful woman dressed in a yellow garment, he handed the spoon to the elf.

"You are fantastic, Shadow! Fantastic!" the elf exclaimed as he put the golden spoon in the large pocket of his coat. "No one saw anything! Your turn now, Darwich Socks! Go! Amuse me!"

The elf untied Amos's chain.

"You want me to steal one of the spoons in the tray over there, is that right?"

"Yes, young braggart!" the elf said, laughing.

"Are all these spoons identical?"

"They are!"

"Very well. I will do as you ask me, but I propose a deal," Amos suggested. "If I fail, you will throw me in the Styx, but if I succeed, you will help me steal something that is of great value to me."

"I refuse!" shouted the elf. "I do not make deals with the likes of you! You are *my* prisoner here."

"All right," Amos answered calmly. "Then throw me in the Styx right now. I am sorry, but I never work for free, and especially not to make a spectacle of myself! I must add that I would succeed—and I would succeed with all eyes upon me. You want to know how? Well, agree to my request! I am Darwich Socks, the greatest thief of the city, and I do not lie!"

The elf narrowed his eyes. "Fine. If you succeed, I will do anything for you," he said, curiosity getting the better of him. "I will even make you an official member of the guild. But I doubt that you can achieve such a feat. I am watching you."

Amos jumped onto a chair. "Stop the music! Stop everything and listen to me!" he shouted at the top of his voice. "Please give me a few seconds of attention!"

The musicians stopped playing and everyone turned toward Amos. The crowd became silent.

"Thank you very much. My name is Darwich Socks and—"

Several people started to laugh and applaud when they heard the strange name.

"Yes, that is my name," Amos went on. "I am a great magician, and with the permission of the master of the house, I will entertain you tonight with one of my famous tricks. Could one of you gentlemen bring me one of the spoons that rests in the center tray?"

The elf nodded his assent and a guard carried out the request. The golden spoon in his hand, Amos pretended to concentrate.

"Beautiful, lovely treasure!" he said. "Go to the one most worthy of you, go to your owner!"

With a theatrical gesture, Amos put the spoon in the pocket of his pants.

"It disappeared!" he said. "It is now in the elf's coat pocket! From my pocket it went to his! Please stand up, Master, and search your coat!"

The elf understood Amos's ruse and knew that he had lost the bet. Biting his lips in rage, he got up. Under the eyes of his guests, he took a golden spoon out of his pocket. It was, of course, the one that Shadow had stolen a moment before.

A thunder of applause rose. Amos bowed a few times.

Amos had in fact stolen the object in front of everyone! He had performed his trick and he had won the game.

"Well," Amos said, satisfied, "there is the proof of my talent. What Shadow did in secret, I did in plain sight. This proves that I am the greatest thief in this city and that I did not lie. Do I have the right to live now?"

"Fine," the elf grumbled. "You are free to go."

"May I have your name?" Amos inquired politely.

"Everyone here has five or six names," the elf answered. "Everything is fake here! Just call me Arkillion. And you, Darwich Socks, is that your real name?"

"No," Amos answered, smiling.

"You see," the elf said, "everything is a lie! I will tell Ougocil that you are now part of our family of thieves. He will be happy to know it! After all, he is the one who recruited you. He will show you our hideouts and most secret spots."

"Thank you. Now, to come back to our agreement—"

The elf answered with a sigh. "You want me to steal something for you, correct?"

"Exactly!" Amos confirmed.

The elf took a sip of some red wine. "What is it that I must steal?"

"The key of Braha!" Amos answered.

The elf choked on his drink and grew pale.

"No, anything . . . anything but that!" he begged.

# —12—

## THE MAHIKUI DESERT

After never-ending weeks of travel, Junos's party finally sighted the desert of Mahikui. Beorf had fully recovered and his wounds had healed well. The long journey had exhausted everyone, the knights as well as the Dogons. They had not encountered any major problems during the endless journey, but the numerous hours on foot had worn everyone out physically and emotionally. A blazing sun had burned the Berrion men's skin. Less accustomed to this suffocating climate than the Dogons, they suffered terribly. Junos, like everyone else, would have given anything for a rainy day or a light refreshing breeze. Only Lolya seemed as fresh as a rose.

"We will stop here for the night," the exhausted lord of Berrion shouted.

"I do not agree," the young queen objected. "I can feel danger. Let's keep going. There is a village a little farther away. We shall be there in merely one hour if we hurry. It will be our last chance to resupply before we really enter the desert."

"I will not take one more step," Junos said. "My men are weary, and your warriors, Lolya, look like wrecks. We are dragging our feet and need some rest. It is here that our day ends."

"It is not wise of you to doubt my word," Lolya answered. "I have the divine gift of sight, and this camp could be the last one of our lives."

"I am tired of your endless discussions, your premonitions, and your visions, young lady!" Junos exploded, growing increasingly impatient. "We are tired! Can you understand that? We have to eat and sleep! We will go to the village tomorrow. We will set up camp here whether you like it or not. Do I make myself clear?"

Lolya gave up. Beorf, hungry as usual, gulped down a ration of dried fruit and a large piece of bread. Then he went to the cart where Amos's body lay and, as always, told him about his day. Talking to his friend gave Beorf the impression that he was keeping Amos alive, maintaining his spirit.

"Will you come with me, Beorf? I am headed to the village," Lolya said, interrupting his monologue. "Junos refuses to go there tonight, but I need information for our itinerary."

"But you told Junos that you had a bad omen," Beorf answered. "Wouldn't you rather ask one of your warriors to go with you?"

"No . . . maybe . . . I do not know how to explain it, Beorf. I am confused. . . . I am pulled between two poles. Something is calling me to the village. I have had strange dreams for almost a week now. Baron Samedi wants to warn me of a danger, but he cannot define it clearly to me. A powerful force is jamming our communication. I want to go to this village as soon as possible."

"Well," Beorf grumbled, "I will accompany you, but I would rather stay here. I am so tired."

"Thank you; you will not regret it," Lolya said, relieved.

On their way, the young queen confided again to the beorite.

"Beorf, do you know of the Elders people?"

"No. Sorry, Lolya, but I have just enough strength left to reach the village. You can tell me your stories later. I'm making a great effort just to remain standing. If you weren't here, I would lie down in the middle of this sandy road."

"Listen to me, it is important!" the young queen insisted.

"Important?" Beorf was beginning to lose patience. "We are in the middle of nowhere, in a scorching desert with a mission to accomplish that I am not certain I understand. Amos is dead, but the reality is that he is not dead! He is supposed to revive, and no one knows how to help him do so! My head is heavy and I am tired. Keep quiet, Lolya. Let us walk in silence."

"I promise you it is important, because I believe that the time has come for me!"

"What time? What are you talking about?" Beorf asked, exasperated.

"I am talking about the Elders' way," Lolya started again. "Walk and listen, so you will not lose any energy. And stop grunting, will you?"

"I am a bear, so I grunt, that is all! You, of the magpie race, you are a chatterbox!"

The young girl laughed, which made Beorf smile. Carried away by Lolya's good humor, he started to giggle uncontrollably. Both of them rolled on the ground with laughter. Suddenly, the young queen stopped.

"What's going on?" Beorf asked, trying to hold his irrepressible laugh.

"We won't have time to go to the village!" Lolya answered, panicked. "It has started!"

"What has started?"

"This is what I wanted to explain to you. It is the way of the Elders. Promise to stay with me whatever happens. Promise me!"

"Yes!" Beorf said. "I promise."

"Listen, then," Lolya went on, trying not to pass out. "I am of the Elders' race, the first inhabitants of this world. We have been hunted by humans and totally eradicated from the face of the earth."

Beorf noticed that Lolya's skin was beginning to tighten

slowly. Her hands were shaking and big drops of sweat appeared on her face.

"I suspected that this would happen! Quick, take me behind the sand dune over there!"

The humanimal's strength came back quickly and he lifted the girl with one arm to carry her behind the dune.

"What you are going to see, Beorf, very few have had the chance to witness," the queen of the Dogons said. "I am afraid. My premonition, my inability to communicate clearly with Baron Samedi, and this call from the village . . . everything is falling into place now. I had to get away from camp. I . . . I am changing now, Beorf. . . . The power of the draconite is working!"

Beorf looked bewildered. "What is a draconite, exactly?"

"Look at the precious stone I have in my throat! The baron put it there. It is a draconite, and it contains the soul of an Elder, the soul of a . . . dragon! You are going to witness the birth of Kur! We, the Elders, disappeared from this world, and Baron Samedi, our god, decided to make us come back to life. We must reclaim the position we used to have on Earth."

"Stop, Lolya, stop now! Let us return to camp so you can be take care of. You are tired and delirious! Come, I will carry you!"

"Let go of me!" the young queen shouted. "Don't you understand anything about what is going on here? I am becoming something else."

Beorf then saw Lolya's face change. Her eyes grew bloodshot and flames danced in her pupils.

"Lolya!" he shouted. "What's happening to you?"

ψ

Junos woke suddenly and emerged from his tent in a hurry. Twilight was coming peacefully, and a soft and unexpected breeze gently brushed his beard. On the horizon, the sun was disappearing gradually, turning the sky a flamboyant red. It was Beorf's voice that had awakened Junos. Or was it a dream? He wasn't sure. The lord of Berrion went to look for the man-bear. All the knights were sleeping like logs. Two Dogons were on duty, seated on the cart where Amos's body lay.

"Excuse me, gentlemen, have you seen Beorf, by any chance?" Junos asked.

Both men shook their heads.

"And Lolya? Do you know where she is?"

He received the same answer from the warriors. Upset, Junos decided to get his horse and look for Beorf. As his foot reached the stirrup, the ground shook and he heard a distant rumble. That was all it took for him to know that something was seriously wrong. An army was galloping at full speed toward the camp! Scanning the horizon, Junos saw the distinctive dust cloud raised by a large cavalry.

"Knights of Equilibrium, get up!" he roared. "Raise your weapons! We're being attacked!"

114

The men were soon ready to fight in spite of the rude awakening. They saw a good hundred warriors rush toward them. Yaune the Purifier was in the lead. He and his men cut down several Dogons with their swords and killed a number of knights. Yaune's larger, mercenary army soon surrounded Junos's camp. There was no way out.

Yaune dismounted and removed his helmet. Confronted with Yaune's vile appearance, Junos stepped back in revulsion. In the past, Yaune, a former Knight of Light, had had rugged good looks. His seductive power had been huge, and people had trusted him easily. The man in front of Junos possessed none of these qualities. With his reptile eye, his scar, and his tattooed forehead, he looked like a monster. He exuded hatred and contempt, resentment and a desire for vengeance. Yaune smiled as he approached the lord of Berrion, who signaled to his men to stay put.

"So, Junos," Yaune said in greeting, "it is a pleasure to meet again the great liberator of Bratel-la-Grande."

"Come to the point," Junos answered dryly. "What do you want of me? What do you want of us?"

"To answer your first question," the fallen knight said, "I want to kill you. What do I want of all of you? Well, I also want to kill you all! But before I do, I will make you suffer!"

"Why? What have I done to deserve such hatred?"

"What have you done?" Yaune shouted. "You have the gall to ask me what you have done? Well, I will tell you," he said more softly. "I was the lord of Bratel-la-Grande. I had an army, men that I could trust, and I ruled as I pleased. Then Karmakas and the gorgons came to destroy me. Fortunately, Junos, the lord of Berrion, came with Amos Daragon to liberate us. But the problem is that you dethroned me and gave my land to Barthelemy. You tattooed the word 'murderer' on my forehead and sent me into exile."

"You were a bad king," Junos answered disdainfully. "Your men revolted against you. You killed and burned many people whom you had unfairly accused of sorcery. You got what you deserved. You should be happy that we spared your life!"

"And you, Junos of Berrion," Yaune said, coming close to the lord, "tell your men to put down their weapons and surrender. We are superior in number and you have no chance of escape. You are my prisoners. Before I chain you like a wild beast, tell me where the warrior girl is." He gave a sinister laugh. "I must cut her throat!"

"She has disappeared," Junos said. "You'll have to look for her."

"Tell your men to surrender now!" Yaune shouted.

With a solemn gesture, Junos signaled to his knights and the remaining Dogon warriors to lay down their weapons. Yaune forced them to undress so that the sun could burn them even more; then he had them chained. Next he climbed onto the cart where Amos's body was lying.

"Clever Amos Daragon," he whispered as he leaned

116

over the boy. "I am glad to see you again. You caused my demise. Well, I am the one who is going to dispatch you into darkness and oblivion, into the nothingness of non-existence. Together we are going to go to the Mahikui desert. We shall find the pyramid and you shall free my army. Afterward I shall open your chest and rip your heart out!"

At dusk, the procession of prisoners began.

# —13—

## THE TRUTH

$A$mos was seated at a table, talking to the elf Arkillion. Shadow, who had taken the elf's physical appearance, was also there, and shared a long bench with Ougocil, the big barbarian.

"How can I explain this simply?" the master of the guild of thieves said. "The key of Braha is a legend, a terrible legend that predicts the end of time, the end of everything. Fortunately, only a few people know about this story."

"I don't understand," Amos said. "The legend says that an elf locksmith created this key at the request of the first magistrate of Braha. Then, because she was not allowed to return to the world of the living, the elf hid the key and bewitched it so that only a living human could get to it. In the realm of the dead, no one can take the key! It is used to open the doors of heaven and hell, is it not? The legend also mentions two formidable guardians."

Arkillion was silent. However, Shadow began to laugh softly, while Ougocil, unable to make sense of this story, scratched his head.

"What are you saying, Darwich Socks?" the elf asked, shaking his head. "Who told you this ridiculous story? I believe you have been fooled, my friend. The key of Braha is not a key, it is an apple!"

"An *apple*?" Amos repeated.

"Yes, an apple!" the elf went on. "I think the time has come for you to drop your mask, Darwich. If you want my help, you must tell me who you really are and what you are doing here in Braha."

Amos realized that his game had lasted long enough. He explained in detail the reason for his presence in the City of the Dead. He disclosed his real name, revealed that he was a mask wearer, and gave a complete account of his first adventure in Bratel-la-Grande. He then spoke of Lolya, the Dogons, Baron Samedi, and Beorf. Then he talked about the ceremony during which the young queen had taken his life, about his trip on the Styx, becoming acquainted with Jerik and Uriel, and, finally, his arrival at the hall of justice. He talked for almost one hour. Arkillion and Shadow did not interrupt him. Ougocil went to sleep rapidly: all this was much too complicated for him.

"Well!" the elf exclaimed at the end of Amos's story. "I

think that you have been duped from the very beginning of your trip. If you don't mind, I will send Shadow to inquire at the hall of justice. He will dig up information."

"Fine with me," Amos said.

"Go, Shadow," Arkillion ordered, "and come back with the truth!"

Shadow disappeared in the blink of an eye.

"You will stay here, Amos," the elf went on. "You will be safe. Ougocil will watch over you . . . when he wakes up. Look at him, sleeping like a baby. I think he no longer knows that he is dead."

"Arkillion, I need to know. What is the key of Braha?"

"I will explain, my friend," the elf answered, trying to gather his thoughts. "The key to Braha comes from a legend that goes back to the time this city was created. When, by common accord, the gods chose the buried city of Braha as a place for the judgment of souls, they planted a tree. That tree, an apple tree that bore only crystal-like fruit, is in fact the tree of eternal life. Whoever eats one of its apples is automatically granted immortality. The key of Braha is the key of life. In fact, it is the great mystery of life for all creatures living on Earth. If you consume one of these apples, you become a god, Amos! The fruit gives immortality to living beings only; that is why the souls of the dead, like you and I, cannot see that tree."

"I understand. . . ."

"In this legend," Arkillion went on, "whoever bites

120

into that fruit will open a door between the realm of the dead and that of the living. Braha will completely empty itself of its ghosts, who will invade Earth to cause the total destruction of the world. A while ago, you mentioned Baron Samedi."

"Yes. Lolya, the young queen of the Dogons, said he was her spiritual guide."

"Baron Samedi is much more than that. He is the supreme god of an extinct race called the Elders. The other gods dismissed him as an unimportant divinity, a minor, second-class servant, but in fact he is very strong. Lolya is his daughter."

For the second time, Amos was stunned. "Lolya is a god's daughter?" he cried. "But how do you know this?"

"I know it because I am an elf. I lived on Earth for thousands of years, and I've been in Braha for just as long. Elves are the repositories of knowledge that humans cannot access."

"In that case, explain to me what the Elders are, this extinct race that had Baron Samedi as supreme god."

"That race lived long before me. When I was born, only a few of them remained. They were hunted and killed by humans."

"Why?"

"Because of their immense wealth. The Elders lived in huge grottos in the heart of mountains and slept on beds made of gold and precious stones. Their heads contained

shiny stones, much in demand by magicians, called draco-
nites. In order to retain their magical power, these stones
had to be stolen from a living Elder. Humans massacred the
Elders to rob them. I was accompanying a group of greedy
humans on one of these expeditions when I lost my life.
Avarice was my flaw, and it caused my death."

"But what are these Elders?"

"They are dragons!" Arkillion said with some confu-
sion. "Lolya is—how do I tell you this?—she is the first
dragon to be reborn on Earth. The gods are again on the
warpath, as you know. Your mission, as you explained it to
me, is to restore equilibrium to the world. Well, the world is
about to experience a severe imbalance. Baron Samedi has
made a choice: he is getting ready to reestablish the reign
of the dragons on Earth. And he will take his revenge over
humans. The gods are using you to accomplish their dark
intentions."

"You mean a god of evil is using me to find the key of
Braha and open the pathway between the world of the living and that of the dead," Amos said, worried. "If I succeed,
I would become a god, and thousands of ghosts would invade Earth to bring about the end of the world! I would survive, but, in so doing, I would cause a cataclysm! If Baron
Samedi had my body brought to the desert of Mahikui, on
top of this pyramid, it is because he is playing a dangerous game and he's using me for his own gains. The baron
expects me to fail in Braha. If I fall short here, in the City

122

of the Dead, he will get rid of me forever, and in a few decades, he will take control of the world with his dragons. Whichever way you look at it, I will cause the destruction of the world. It is hopeless! I am done for! There is no way out. . . ."

A heavy silence fell over the room. Arkillion, his chin resting in his hands, was thinking, while a deep feeling of helplessness invaded Amos. Ougocil chose that instant to wake up.

"You have to erase everything," he said, yawning wide. "You have to go backward and begin all over again!"

"Quiet!" Arkillion said. "Can't you see we are trying to think?"

Amos jumped up. He threw his arms around Ougocil and kissed his forehead.

"You're a genius, dear Ougocil!" he said excitedly. "A real genius!"

# —14—

## THE BEAST OF FIRE

Beorf could not believe his eyes. A few meters away from him, Lolya was transforming into a dragon. She became immense, gigantic! The young queen's skin melted slowly. The bones of her skull moved, gradually taking on a larger shape. Wings sprouted from her back, and strong claws replaced her fingers. Fright paralyzed the humanimal. Unable to move even one finger, he remained motionless, close to the beast, powerless to flee. A strong smell of musk came from the dragon, who was as black as ebony and covered with scales. Its mouth was huge; its teeth looked like monumental stalactites and stalagmites. It turned toward Beorf.

"I kept you alive, Beorf Bromanson, so that you would witness the resurrection of the Elders and tell humans to submit to the new order that Earth is going to know," the dragon said. "Lolya is no more. My name is Kur, and soon I shall be the master of this world. Lolya was my wrapping, my egg, my milk tooth. I was growing inside her, feeding her with my powers. In the Elders' language, Kur means 'mountain.' Soon I shall give birth to a race of inferior creatures, the dragons of the plain. They will be smaller than me, and humans will recognize them by their vivid scales and pointed crest. They will open the way for the world to welcome the Elders. Humans will submit and become our servants. Like the Dogons, they all will sacrifice their lives to feed us. In ancient times, Nanda and Upananda, the two guardians of the gold column that is now called the cosmic axis, lived in Lake Anavatapta. Humans killed them out of greed. The gold column was desecrated. From that day on, Earth's axis changed and terrible cataclysms occurred. That is what humans are capable of doing! In the past, each mountain had a dragon and peace existed between all creatures. We were the masters, the judges and the lawyers, and we governed by fear. We simply forgot that humans can overcome fear when they are driven by their thirst for power and wealth. We were extremely rich. We had gold beds, mountains of precious stones! Humans stole everything! Why? Just to scatter the bounty around the world. This time, no one will rob us with impunity!"

Beorf listened, openmouthed and wide-eyed. The sight of the monstrous creature made his heart beat madly and his legs shake. He couldn't think clearly. The fear he felt confused him, so he kept listening to the dragon.

"Azi Dahaka was chained and tortured for nine thousand years by generations of humans who wanted him to reveal where his treasure was hidden. He never spoke. He never said anything! His silence and his prolonged agony will be rewarded today. It is in his lair, on his gold bed, that I will prepare the rebirth of my people. I will become larger than Rouimon, the blind dragon who killed humans just by growling. He, who was cut into pieces by the luminous swords of celestial spirits during the last war of the gods, will be proud of me."

From the moment he started to talk, Kur had swallowed hundreds of large stones. On the edge of the Mahikui desert, rocks were rich in phosphor. This gave Kur, and all dragons, the ability to spit fire. The phosphorous stones dissolved quickly into powerful acids in the stomachs of the beasts, creating a flammable gas. Dragons just had to burp for the gas to catch fire when it came in contact with air. This jet of fire could reach a distance of six hundred feet and come close to temperatures of two thousand degrees. Kur was getting ready for a bloody attack.

"Go!" the dragon told Beorf. "I won't keep you! I saved your life and I won't take it back. I know that your race of man-beasts, the beorites, is almost extinct. I take pity on endangered races. So I am sparing your life. I also want you to tell what you saw and heard. Make me a legend in this world! Talk about my greatness and splendor to everybody!

Consider yourself lucky, Beorf Bromanson; you have come close to a dragon without losing your life. Now good-bye, young bear! The new master of the world bids you farewell!"

Kur swallowed a last stone and spread his wings. In a move as strong as it was delicate, the dragon took to the air. He flapped his wings a few times and disappeared into the clouds, leaving Beorf alone on the edge of the desert.

When Beorf returned to his senses, night had come. He had the strong feeling that this incredible adventure was a dream—a nightmare that left only vague images. Beorf quickly morphed into his bear form and ran toward Junos's camp. He worried that the men of Berrion might have been incinerated by the dragon. He had to go and see for himself. He needed to know that Lolya had really been transformed into a dragon and that he had not dreamed it all.

At the camp, there was no one in sight. The tents and carts were still there. On the ground, Beorf saw the bodies of five knights. Armor, weapons, and all the transport equipment were spread on the ground in great disorder. There had been a battle here, but not with a dragon. Looking closely at the wounds of the dead knights, Beorf recognized Yaune's signature cuts. He had been on the receiving end of the same poisonous strokes. It was now obvious to Beorf that Yaune had attacked the camp, killed a few men, and made prisoners of the remaining troops. Amos's body had also disappeared. There was no doubt that Yaune the Purifier was headed toward the pyramid of the Mahikui desert.

The man-bear rapidly headed toward the village that Lolya had said was not very far, about one hour's walk from the camp. Yet when Beorf reached the village, it was already too late. Kur had arrived before him: houses had been burned from top to bottom and were still smoking. The bodies of men, women, and children were charred and strewn on the ground. The beast had spared no one as it celebrated its rebirth.

Changing back to his human form, Beorf searched the debris without success. There were no survivors. Even domesticated animals lay dead on the ground. Beorf went to the well to quench his thirst, but the contaminated water was no longer drinkable. The beorite was at an impasse. He was faced with two options: either he could retrace his steps and obey Kur's orders by announcing the rebirth of the dragons and the end of the world, or he could hurry into the desert to try to find Junos, the pyramid, and Amos's body. If he chose the latter option, he knew he would have to confront Yaune or, even worse, meet the dragon again.

Beorf took a deep breath and looked at the desert that spread endlessly before him.

"For someone who hates sand, I am blessed!" he said loudly as he wiped his forehead.

And, still thirsty, Beorf rushed into the desert.

These past few days Yaune had progressed into the desert with his mercenaries and his prisoners. Resting during the day and traveling at night, Yaune followed the plan set out by Seth. The men of Berrion and the Dogons had hardly eaten or drunk anything since the day they were taken prisoners. They were on foot, whereas their captors rode strong camels. Yaune had swapped horses for the camels, which were better suited to the arid area. The top of the buried pyramid was now in sight. Yaune called Junos over.

"What's to be done with Amos's body when we reach the pyramid?" he asked the lord.

"I don't know," Junos said, barely able to speak due to his weariness and thirst. "Even if I did, I would not tell you!"

"Oh, you will talk! You will talk, I am sure of that!" Yaune answered, kicking Junos with his boots.

Yaune dismissed the lord of Berrion, then took a sphere out of a bag that Seth had offered him before his journey began. The sphere help him control his army of specters. Its magic power would subject all the ghosts to his wishes. Yaune would be the uncontested and indisputable master of the world. He kissed the small crystal ball and carefully put it back in the bag.

A few hours later, when he arrived at the pyramid, Yaune asked for Junos again. The lord of Berrion fell on his knees at Yaune's feet.

"Tell me now what must be done!" Yaune shouted. "We have Amos's body, the pyramid, and the desert! What is missing?"

"I don't know, Yaune, I don't know . . . ," Junos managed to say with difficulty. His lips were more parched than ever.

"Very well, you know nothing! You are taking this trip just for the fun of it, then. Well, I'm going to make you talk! I swear I will. . . ."

Yaune motioned to one of his mercenaries, who unchained one of the Berrion men and forced him to kneel in front of Yaune, very close to Junos. With one swipe of his sword, Yaune cut the knight's head off. Junos cried out.

"What will it be?" Yaune said, calmly wiping the blood from his sword onto the sand. "One of your knights just died because of you. Will you save the others? You speak and they live; you do not speak and I behead them one by one. I repeat my question: tell me what is to be done now?"

"Lolya," Junos said. "The young queen of the Dogons knows the way to open the door."

"Bring me another brave knight!" Yaune shouted as he looked at his mercenaries.

"No!" Junos cried. "I will tell you what I know, everything I know."

"At last, you're becoming more reasonable," Yaune said, laughing. "Go on, I am listening!"

"Baron Samedi, the spiritual guide of Lolya, spoke to us. He said to come to the Mahikui desert and find the tip of the pyramid, which sticks out of the ground. Lolya was supposed to activate the mechanism that opens a secret door. We were to place Amos's body in the center of the pyramid so that he could come back to life and accomplish his mission. We had two months to succeed. Everything was to be in place for the next eclipse of the sun."

Suddenly, a voice rang out of nowhere.

"Good, Junos! You've learned your lesson well," the deep and somber voice said.

Yaune looked all around him. "Who are you?" he shouted. "Come out and show yourself!"

"At your peril!" the voice answered.

Behind the tip of the pyramid, a shadow emerged. Tall and powerful, Kur the dragon appeared. The Dogons immediately kneeled and began to pray fervently. Their arms to the sky, they started an old religious song. Yaune and Junos looked at each other in disbelief. The mercenaries started to panic and tried to flee. Kur inhaled deeply, then blew forcefully in their direction. The men caught on fire and fell to the ground.

"In just one breath I wiped out your men," Kur said, looking at Yaune. "Impressive, no?"

Yaune cleared his throat. "What do you want of me, dragon?" he said, trying to sound threatening. "I warn you to leave. Or you will be subjected to my ire!"

"How brave you are, little snake!" Kur answered calmly. "What I want is very simple. I want to become the master of this world, just like you! I know that you are Seth's servant. As for me, I serve Baron Samedi. We are both servants of a god, but only one of us will survive this encounter. You want to enter the pyramid? Well, I am opening the door."

Three huge stones suddenly moved and a door appeared in the wall.

"But to go in," the dragon went on, "you will have to kill me."

"Seth will not appreciate this intrusion into his business," Yaune declared, gripping his sword tightly.

Kur flapped his enormous wings. "The mask wearer must not find the key of Braha. If his soul reconnects with his body and falls into the trap that you and Seth have set for him, you will lead the greatest army of specters Earth has ever known. This cannot happen because Baron Samedi is preparing the rebirth of the Elders' reign. The world will be his, not Seth's!"

"You played your hand well, you and your baron," Yaune answered. "Now the moment of truth has come."

As the two enemies confronted each other, Junos crawled away and managed to untie his men. The Dogons were still praying with the same intensity. Junos quickly slung Amos's body over his shoulders, then motioned to his knights, who jumped onto the camels and took off. This commotion attracted the dragon's attention.

The lord of Berrion took advantage of this diversion to throw himself headfirst through the opening of the pyramid, dragging Amos's body with him. The door closed behind them. In the dark Junos tumbled down stone steps, but he never let go of the mask wearer's remains.

After a long descent, Junos and Amos landed noisily in a dusty room filled with hundreds of spiderwebs. Junos lay on his back in utter agony. He took a deep breath. After feeling to determine if he had suffered any broken bones, he confirmed his fear: he had broken two ribs and a leg. In the almost-total darkness, the lord managed to find Amos's body.

"Well, the dragon will not come to look for us here," he whispered. "It is too big. The door is closed. I believe that we have nothing to fear. I think that—"

Junos passed out before he could finish his sentence. The journey, the hunger, the thirst, the pain, and the intensity of these last few minutes had consumed all his energy.

# —15—

## SHADOW'S REPORT

Amos spent several days in the lair of the thieves' guild before he saw Shadow enter his apartment. The shape-shifter moved slowly in his direction. He did not speak. But as he came into contact with the mask wearer, his gaseous form melted into Amos's anatomy. At that moment, everything became clear in Amos's mind.

Shadow had made inquiries within the hall of justice. Taking the shape of one employee and then another, that of an object or of a statue, he had heard conversations and spied on judges and now understood the nature of the plot hatched against Amos. Just as Arkillion had suspected, Amos was facing an intricate plot in which he was only a pawn. Seth had come up with a plan to give Yaune an army with which to conquer the world in his name. When he had kidnapped Forseti, the god of justice, he had known full well that the doors of Braha would close.

Ganhaus, Uriel, and Jerik were also part of the plot. Seth had naively hoped that Amos would find the key of Braha and open the pathway between the dead and the living. But Magistrate Ganhaus had other ideas. He wanted to keep the key of Braha for himself and become a god. That was why Jerik followed Amos's every step. He was to inform Ganhaus of Amos's slightest move and direct the mask wearer toward the key of Braha as soon as Forseti had finally been broken. At the right time, Uriel would get rid of Amos and bring the apple of light—the key of Braha—to his brother.

Within this scheme, where each of the protagonists worked for his own interest, yet another plot had hatched. The snake god had not foreseen that Baron Samedi, who for centuries had wanted to bring the order of the dragons back to Earth, would use Seth's plan to achieve his own ends. From the time the dragons had disappeared, the baron had patiently executed all the simple and menial tasks that the merciful gods of good had given him—managing the world's cemeteries and the handling of the dead souls that arrived in Braha. The fallen god had helped Seth in bringing Amos to the City of the Dead. The baron needed time before Kur's birth, the first of his new dragons. In fact, he relied on Amos's failure to be rid of him. He was killing three birds with one stone! He would leave Amos to rot in Braha; send Kur to kill Seth's servant on Earth, Yaune the Purifier; and give birth to a new menace over the world. The war of the gods was also a war between the gods of evil.

Having finished his report, Shadow separated his body from that of Amos's. Arkillion the elf entered the room at that moment.

"So, are you satisfied with Shadow's work?" he asked.

Amos nodded. "Yes, very pleased. But tell me, Arkillion: Why is it that the gods do not confront each other directly? Why do they always have to use terrestrial beings to do their bidding?"

"Simple, my friend!" the elf answered. "Because they are immortal! A direct confrontation does not make much sense to them. They would not gain anything from such a fight because they are indestructible. Instead, Earth is a huge chessboard on which they play a merciless game. They make up the rules as they play, and of course each player wants to be the winner. On one side, there is good; on the other, evil; and between the two, there is us: the elves, the humans, and also the dragons, the dwarfs, the goblins, the fairies, and all the others creatures of the world. We are all here to play their game, to fight their fights, to sacrifice our lives like pawns. Your mission, as a mask wearer, is not to make one or the other win; your mission is to stop the game so that the world can live in peace!"

"Yes, I see what you mean," Amos answered, emphasizing

each of his words. "And I think I know how to stop this game. I need your help, though. Will you help me?"

Arkillion smiled wide. "Shadow and I have been waiting a long time for a little bit of fun," he said, rubbing his hands in delight. "Ougocil will also be glad to give us a hand."

"Come close, my friends," Amos began. "This is what we are going to do. . . ."

Jerik arrived in a hurry. Amos was waiting for him, near a big monastery right beside the deserted public square.

"Where were you?" the secretary asked nervously. "Everybody was looking for you . . . uh . . . these past few days. . . . We . . . how do I say? . . . we were worried. An elf . . . came to tell me that you were waiting for me here. . . . What is going on?"

"Do you have the ten gold coins that the elf asked you to bring?" Amos asked.

"Yes . . . yes . . . but I would like to understand . . . I mean . . . ," Jerik said as he handed the purse of coins to Amos, "how . . . these ten . . . how is this money going to help you?"

"Thank you," Amos said, smiling. "You betrayed me, Jerik. I know the full story now. I know that the key of Braha is an apple of light, I know that Ganhaus wants it for himself, I know of Seth's plan, and I also know that Uriel is waiting for the right time to throw me into the Styx. Unfortunately for you, everything ends here!"

"But . . . but . . . how can you know?" Jerik mumbled.

At that moment, Shadow took on the shape of the secretary. He was identical in every way—even down to the head held under his arm.

"What is this?" Jerik asked anxiously.

"It's my turn to play now!" Amos answered. "Your part in this game is over!"

With a swift and powerful kick, Amos booted Jerik's head out from under his arm. The head flew into the air and fell in the center of the square.

"But what's happening?" the secretary cried. "What . . . is happening?"

"Careful or you'll be bitten!" Amos told him, laughing.

Three ferocious, sharp-toothed black dogs materialized in the square. Before Jerik had time to react, his head was flying like a balloon between the paws of one dog and the fangs of another. Amos turned toward Shadow.

"Now that you look like Jerik, go to the palace and try to find out where the tree of eternal life is located," he said. "Seth has probably been able to make Forseti, the god of justice, talk. It is Jerik who was to direct me to the key of Braha. Come back with this information. In the meantime, I have a few other things to settle."

Shadow left immediately. Amos grabbed Jerik's headless body by the hand and walked toward the park where he had met Angess. Without its head, the secretary's skeleton followed Amos without protest. On the same bench as during Amos's first visit to the park, Angess was waiting for Peten, her lost love. Her father's sword was still stuck through her neck, and she was looking desperately in every direction. Her sorrow was obvious, her eyes filled with tears. Amos pushed Jerik's body close to her.

"There is Peten, dear Angess," Amos said. "I found him for you. The thought of never seeing you again made him lose his head. But it is Peten, I promise you."

"Peten! Peten!" Angess cried, bursting with joy. "Here you are at last! Thank you, young man, thank you for everything. My heart is free now and my soul is at peace. Thank you again!"

Angess took hold of one of Jerik's hands and covered it with kisses. Then she led him away.

"Not bad!" Amos said to himself. "I still have another matter to settle!"

The mask wearer headed to the street where Vincenc, the seven-foot skeleton, lived. Once there, he took the purse that Jerik had given him and threw it up at the giant.

"Take this, my friend," he said. "There are enough coins to buy back your bones from the anatomy professor. I hope you come across him soon."

The skeleton jumped up and down with joy and thanked Amos warmly. Amos rubbed his hands, laughing and happy. He turned to go back to the thieves' lair—and found himself facing a wall. Looking around, he noticed that the entire city had disappeared. He took a few steps back. That was when he realized that he was now at the foot of the great pyramid of Braha.

A strong light appeared in front of his eyes, cutting a door in the rock face. A magnificent angel flew out the door. It had very long blond hair, luminous green eyes, powerful white wings, and an armored tunic covered with gold and precious stones. Its skin was as white as snow, its teeth perfectly aligned, and its face smooth. It was taller than Vincenc's skeleton and its muscles were oversized. It wore a large crystal sword in its belt.

Amos was startled to see such a sight.

"Are you the one looking for the key of Braha?" the angel asked.

"Yes," Amos answered politely. "I am."

"Well, you are now at the door that leads to the tree of life," the celestial guardian went on.

"How did I get here?" Amos asked softly.

"To reach this door, there is no path, nor road. One arrives here only through merit. First, one must want to find the tree of life. Then one has to do three significant good deeds that bring peace and happiness to souls in distress. You gave the monastery's dogs the head of a treacherous individual, someone who deserved punishment. In so doing, you have liberated three men from their curse. They had to punish another thief in order to find rest. You found a Peten for Angess and she is happy now. It was your last generous deed, for Vincenc, that dispatched you here. Through your generosity and desire to help others, you found the road that leads to godliness."

"Thank you, but . . . what . . . what do I have to do now, to enter?"

"Your body is already in the pyramid," the angel answered. "Technically, you have entered. To restore you to life, you must solve three riddles. These three riddles will determine your wisdom and your spirit. One bad answer and you will return to Braha. It will be impossible for you to come before me again. One has only a single chance to become a god! If you succeed, your body will be given back to you and you will face another guardian. This one is a powerful demon who protects the tree of life. He will also test you."

"Very well," Amos said. "Ask your questions, I am ready."

"Here is the first riddle: What embraces the entire world and never meets anyone similar to it?"

Amos thought for a few seconds. "It is the sun!" he answered. "It circles the entire world and never meets anyone looking like it."

"Correct!" the guardian exclaimed. "You possess the steely confidence of a god, young man. The second riddle now: What feeds its little ones and swallows the big ones?"

"It is the sea," Amos said, without hesitation. "It feeds men and swallows rivers."

"Once more, you surprise me," the angel declared with

admiration. "My last riddle: What is the half-black and half-white tree?"

Amos had to think hard. He knew that the tree was surely a metaphor for life, a symbol. He thought about the tree of life, about immortality and his mission as mask wearer.

"The tree that is half black and half white is the human soul," he answered finally. "It grows in every man and has, like the passing days, a white side linked to good and a black side linked to evil."

"Your first test is a success," the angel answered. "I am now going to reunite your soul with your body."

# —16—

## BEORF'S HUNGER

Beorf had run without respite across the desert. He was thirstier and hungrier than ever—which was typical of beorites. Deprived of food, man-bears are prone to violence and depression, and are known to swallow anything that comes their way. Beorf gobbled two small lizards and almost gulped down a scorpion. But the scorpion was faster than Beorf and quickly dashed off. In this desert of sand and rocks, there was nothing to eat or drink. No plants and no oases, only dunes and piles of stones.

After a while, the humanimal inhaled the sweet aroma of warm chestnuts and vegetable soup. In his nostrils, whiffs of cinnamon, mint, and rosemary mixed with the scent of ripe fruit. But an intoxicating odor dominated everything else: that of grilled meat! Beorf imagined it juicy and perfectly cooked. Growing dizzy from this delicious attack on his senses, he lost his balance and fell facefirst on the ground. He was so hungry! Gathering his strength, he began to climb the dune toward the banquet. It required all his strength to reach the top of the sand dune, but he made it. When he saw a table laden with food, the humanimal cried with pleasure and threw himself on a juicy piece of meat.

As he ate, Beorf watched the fight between Kur and Yaune the Purifier close by. It was a grand show.

Next to the buried pyramid of Mahikui, both combatants—strengthened by the power of their gods—were fighting with devastating ardor. Yaune was no more than a scorched body, but still he waved his sword. His skeleton was visible under his burned skin. His muscles had been torn and only a few pieces of his armor were still in place. His hairless head and beardless face were horrible to watch. Only his reptile eye—Seth's gift—remained open and whole.

In spite of his pitiful condition, Yaune was attacking the dragon with ferocity. The monster was spitting fire at him, but the knight was not giving up. Kur was receiving numerous blows that tore at a good number of his scales. The monster was covered with the dark blood running from his wounds. Without stopping, Kur kept hurling blows with his tail and jaws. The knight sometimes fell, but he always managed to hurt Kur with his sharp blade.

At times, the two adversaries withdrew a distance from each other to catch their breath and regain some strength. Kur, in one flap of his wings, lifted himself to land a little farther away. The beast bent and swallowed a huge quantity of phosphorus stones. Yaune took advantage of the break to try to fix his armor. The dragon licked his wounds at the end of the pause. Relieved of the pain for a little while, the beast of fire returned to fight. Yaune drew his sword and rushed at the monster.

The knight knew that dragons had a fatal weakness, a chink in their armor. Somewhere on their body a single scale was missing. The exact spot differed from dragon to dragon. It could be under the tail, behind the head, at an elbow, or on the back. The vulnerable spot was a dragon's greatest secret, and of course, a dragon never revealed its weakness.

Yaune looked for this flaw, slashing Kur's body with strong blows. He was striking the dragon's legs, toes, neck, and arms, hoping to hit on the dragon's Achilles' heel. The knight, now invested with Seth's power, knew that he could never triumph over the dragon by himself. His poisonous sword had little effect on the creature. The dragon's black blood was a more potent poison.

Kur also knew that the knight was indestructible. Yaune was no longer a man: he was a lich—a type of undead creature endowed with immeasurable power. Representing a god on Earth, the lich was insensitive to the elements.

Kur's fire, as scorching as it was, could not overcome Yaune. His god had invested a new power in the knight, and no blow, whether from Kur's tail or his claws, would be able to destroy him. Only the magic of a very powerful sorcerer could stop or hurt him.

Conscious of their invulnerability, the two adversaries kept fighting with the same frenzied intensity. The confrontation was no longer between a dragon and a knight, but between Seth and Baron Samedi. The gods were evaluating each other through their creatures, and each hoped to take advantage of the other's weakness to win. They were gambling the world's future in this desert. The new order would be that of the dragons or that of the specters. Either men and all of Earth's creatures would become the slaves of the Elders, or they would join the lich's army in death. Both servants of the gods fought mercilessly for the glory of evil.

Stupefied but still eating, Beorf watched the showdown. He had never seen such a display of force and brutality. Kur was ferociously spitting fire on Yaune, who, in spite of his burns, was hitting the dragon with all his might, still without being able to cut deeply into its scales. It was a fight equal to the greatest battles ever fought.

Once his hunger was satisfied, the humanimal came back to his senses and wondered what this table covered with food was doing in the desert. He looked around and realized that there was no table, no food, and no banquet.

No trace of candles, or servants, or soup or warm chestnuts. Beorf was seated on the ground and was in fact chewing a piece of meat. He was eating *something*, but what? In horror, he realized that he had eaten the thigh of one of Yaune's mercenaries killed by the dragon. That was what had smelled so strongly of barbecued meat. That was what had created the mirage of a banquet and driven him here!

His empty stomach and imagination had betrayed him. Beorf had eaten human flesh. For a humanimal, this crime against nature had dramatic consequences: he would lose his humanity. From now on the beorite would be prisoner of his animal form. Beorf would become a bear and never again walk on two legs. His throat would only let out growls. No more comfortable home for him, no more bed or games with friends. He would have to hunt to feed himself, fight other bears to defend his territory, and always live in fear of hunters. It was too late to turn back the clock.

Beorf started to cry. As his tears fell, he felt his fur grow slowly. Against his will, his head and limbs changed. Permanent claws were growing at the end of his fingers. A jaw with solid fangs took the place of his mouth. Two round ears came out to replace his human ones. In a few minutes, his body had changed completely.

Still seated in front of the cadaver and howling his misfortune, Beorf felt his conscience gradually disappearing. His parents' faces, his cottage in the forest of Bratel-la-Grande, his meetings with Amos, all that had made him human began to fade away. He forgot his childhood games, forgot Junos and the city of Berrion. His last thought was of Medusa, the young gorgon he had spent a few days with in his parents' grotto, at the time of the conquest of the land of the Knights of Light by the magician Karmakas.

Medusa had sacrificed her life for him. Now he was going to forget her, and no one, except Amos, would be able to tell his story. Everything darkened in his mind.

The young bear raised his head and looked around. In spite of his hunger and the morsel of meat at his feet, the animal got scared. The dragon's fire raised a terrible fright in him and he took off in the desert sands. Beorf, the always-cheerful plump boy, was gone forever.

A solar eclipse then plunged the whole area into darkness.

# —17—

## AMOS'S AWAKENING

Amos's eyes popped open. His soul had found his body again. For the first time in a long while, he could breathe wholly. His heart was beating and his blood was running in his veins. Unable to move yet, Amos looked around him. The angel had warned him not to panic, that it would take a few minutes for the numbness to leave his limbs.

The mask wearer lay on a large stone table in the center of a room that he had never seen before. Hundreds of candles were lit around him. The walls were painted with strange signs representing the position of the stars. There were also magical formulas, hieroglyphs, and texts written in a foreign language. A ray of light, no larger in diameter than a coin, came into the room through a hole cut in the stone ceiling. This beam of light fell on one of the walls, landing exactly over a drawing representing a moon. Feeling stronger now, Amos managed to sit up.

At his feet, Amos saw a bloodied man stretched out. The man breathed with difficulty. Amos recognized his friend Junos. He crouched and listened to Junos's heart. It was still beating, but weakly. Amos raised Junos's head and tried to make him regain consciousness.

"Junos, it's me . . . Amos. Can you hear me?"

"Amos?" the lord of Berrion whispered, trying to open his eyes. He coughed. "I'm glad to see that you're well. You won't believe me, but . . . I saw angels . . . real angels. . . . They lit candles and then . . . they took your body next to mine. I saw your soul fly and return to your body. It was so beautiful!"

"I believe you, Junos," Amos answered, smiling. "Only, if you had seen all that I've seen, you would find your angels quite plain."

"Ah!" the lord sighed. "I would love to hear that story, but I don't think I have enough time left."

"What happened?" Amos asked anxiously. "Who did this to you?"

"It would be long . . . too long to explain," Junos answered. "I think that my time has come. . . . I think the end is near. . . ."

"Tell me how to get out of here!" Amos cried. "We'll find someone who can take care of you!"

"I won't get out of here . . . I know it!" Junos went on,

coughing up large blood clots. "Outside, there is an enormous dragon and a demented knight. Let me be. Do what you have to do and don't bother about me. You saved me once in the woods of Tarkasis . . . but this time, you cannot!"

"I won't leave you, Junos!"

"Listen, Amos," Junos said slowly but sternly. "My men and I brought you . . . here to accomplish a mission. Do not disappoint me, do not disappoint us! Several lost their lives . . . in . . . in this adventure. Be worthy of our trust and finish your task. I'm with you, we're all with you. Go! Go . . . now!"

Junos closed his eyes. Amos bent over his friend's chest and realized that the lord of Berrion's heart had stopped beating. He wiped a tear from his eye.

"I'm fed up with all this! Fed up with all these games, lies, and pain," Amos said. "Do humans and other creatures of Earth have to pay so dearly when the gods are at war?"

He looked at Junos.

"I swear, Junos, that I shall save you once more. I'm going to start all this from the beginning and I will pull strings this time. So long, my friend! We will meet again soon!"

As he looked around, Amos saw the diagonal ray of light gradually weaken. Outside the pyramid, the solar eclipse was at its peak. Once the light had disappeared, a door opened in one of the walls. The heavy stones moved to reveal another staircase, this one descending even deeper into the structure. Amos grabbed a few candles and went toward the steps. Hundreds of thick spiderwebs obscured the way down.

Reunited with his body, Amos concentrated and extended his hand. A powerful wind rose from his fingers and the spiderwebs blew away. The passage was clear. Guided by his candles, Amos entered the long corridor.

The walls surrounding the stairs were slimy. Amos smelled a bitter stench and quickly covered his nose. Thousands of spiders were crawling on the stones around him. It was obvious that this passage had not been used in a long time. Amos descended the spiraling steps, going deeper and deeper into the center of the pyramid. He thought about Shadow, Arkillion, and Ougocil. They were no doubt wondering what had happened to him. Amos had asked Shadow to continue his inquiry in the hall of justice. He would never hear his report. The elf and the big barbarian had outlined a plan to eliminate Uriel and his brother, the magistrate Ganhaus. The mask wearer had found true friends in Braha, friends who were ready to help him, and he was upset not to be able to communicate with them. He would have loved to send them a message, tell them that he was alive and well. But now that he was back in the world of the living, he was completely cut off from the City of the Dead.

The steps stopped in front of an arched door that opened onto a large empty room. As soon as Amos passed the threshold, a torch lit up each corner of the room. He saw a strange creature get up from a chair in front of a huge metal door. The monster had a goat's head crowned with a long mane of thick, dirty hair, and antelope-like horns. Its elongated body was gray, hairy, and hunchbacked. Its legs ended in strong horse hooves. Its chest was bare, and it wore metallic pants that resembled the armor of a knight. This garment reflected the light of the torches, sending off red glints through the whole room. A large gold key, finely chiseled, dangled around the creature's neck.

The creature slowly picked up a big scythe that was resting against the wall, and then came to the center of the room. Amos took a few steps back. He did not know what to expect and looked calmly at the scene while trying to analyze each detail. The monster took a combat position.

"I am the Phooka, guardian of the door," the creature said in a hoarse and bleating voice. "Whoever wants to become a god must first fight me. Be prepared to die, young man!"

Amos knew that he would not be able to win. His powers as mask wearer were limited to the raising of the wind—and in a limited way since he had only one of the power stones. Too weak to create a hurricane or a tornado, his chances of overcoming the Phooka were slight. Only his quick thinking could get him out of this situation.

Amos stepped forward. "We will fight later. First I have

to make sure that you are truly the guardian of the tree of life."

"I am," the creature answered, slightly annoyed. "I don't have to give you any proof, only the key. I have been chosen by the great council of six hells to guard this door. You triumphed over the angel, the first guardian. Now you must destroy me to claim your divine status. I have been waiting for one such as you for years. *En garde!*"

"If you have been waiting that long, you can wait a few more minutes," Amos answered, doing his best to hide his nervousness. "I want to make sure that the key you are keeping is the right one. I've gone through many tests, heard many lies, and I am wary."

"Only when I am dead will you have the key!" the Phooka cried in anger. "Prepare to die!"

"Stop threatening me and listen!" Amos ordered. "I demand to know if yours is the right key and if you are truly the guardian of these premises. I cannot escape, as you can see! You would easily catch me in the stairs. I have only my word, and you can trust me. Wait, I will offer you a deal. . . ."

Amos took one of the candles that he was carrying and put it firmly on the ground in front of him.

"Listen to my offer," he went on. "Hand me the key so I can check to see if it is the right one. When the light of this candle goes off by itself, I will give you back the key and we will fight."

"All right," the guardian grumbled as he removed the key from his neck. "You can keep it as long as the candle burns."

"I have only my word," Amos said, hoping that his ruse would work. "I swear to the gods that I will give you back the key as soon as the light of the candle goes off by itself. Do you swear to respect this agreement?"

"I swear," Phooka answered. "I swear by the gods of hell and the power of darkness to let you have the key until the light of this candle stops burning. I also swear to kill you afterward!"

"We shall see about that then. Give me the key now."

The guardian smiled a vicious smile. The Phooka had been waiting for this moment for so many years that waiting a few more minutes did not make much difference. The creature had detected nervousness and fear in Amos's voice. The mask wearer was unsure of himself. Feeling confident, the guardian handed the key to Amos.

Amos took it and put it around his neck. Very calmly, he bent toward the ground and blew out the candle.

"What are you doing?" the Phooka asked, both curious and angry. "You haven't even looked at the key!"

"I will keep it," Amos answered firmly. "It is mine now."

"What are you talking about? We had an agreement. You were to keep the key until the light of the candle went off on its own."

"Yes, but I just blew it out. Therefore it did not go off by itself."

"You tricked me! You tricked me!" the Phooka shouted. "I'll kill you!"

"You cannot!" Amos answered bravely. "You promised to kill me after you got the key back. I did not trick you. I overcame you! I have the key and the promise you made is protecting me from you. Move away, I must go and bite into an apple of light!"

"It is out of the question!" the creature shouted. "I'm certainly not going to abandon my post. I've waited too long for the day someone would have the strength and courage to stand before me."

The Phooka raised his scythe. As he was about to strike out at Amos, the guardian suddenly turned to stone. He was now as still as a statue. Amos was victorious.

The mask wearer approached the metal door, wondering how he could open it. It looked very heavy. Huge hinges supported it on both sides. In its center was a very small lock. Amos pushed the key into the keyhole and gave it one full turn. He took a step back. On the door, these words appeared in letters of fire:

*The one who dies and comes back to life,*
*The one who sails the Styx*
*And finds his way,*
*The one who answers the angel*

*And vanquishes the devil*
*Is the one who will find the key of Braha.*

The ground began to shake. The tremor was concentrated inside the room, growing stronger, until the two walls surrounding the door exploded. Torrents of water came rushing in. The room would be totally flooded in a few seconds. Amos would have to swim underwater to reach the surface. Could he hold his breath long enough? He could swim, but not extraordinarily well.

Thinking fast, Amos raised his arms and created a powerful draft that pushed the water away from him. At the same time, the draft created an air bubble around him. This bubble swirled about in the water, becoming firmer. It was now puncture-proof. Amos kept concentrating and felt that he was moving. Just as air always finds its way to the surface of water, the mask wearer knew that he was saved. The bubble moved out of the room and began its climb.

As he looked around, Amos saw bodies and faces in the water. Their skin was green and seemed sticky. All these strange creatures had long brown hair that floated and undulated around their heads. Their protruding eyes looked like those of frogs, and their green sharp teeth did not inspire confidence. There were hundreds of them. They moved slowly and calmly watched Amos go by. Scared by these strange creatures, he closed his eyes to remain focused.

He absolutely did not want the bubble to burst. Swimming in the same waters as these aquatic monsters was out of the question. As he contemplated this unappealing prospect, he felt that he was about to emerge.

Opening his eyes, he lost his focus and found himself in water. He noticed a small island nearby. Never had Amos swum so fast to reach the shore! The very thought of the green creatures grabbing at his feet and dragging him to the bottom gave him the strength and speed he needed.

He breathed deeply when he set foot on the island. In front of him, dead center, was the tree of life of Braha. It had a colossal trunk and immense branches that covered the whole sky with its foliage. Its apples of light formed luminous constellations. What Amos thought was an island was in fact the tree itself. The mask wearer was standing on its roots.

Looking down, he noticed that these roots plunged deep underwater.

The green creatures with protruding eyes were swimming under the tree and feeding it. They took turns diving into the depths of the water, bringing back a thick, muddy paste between their hands. They covered the roots with the brown mud, then dove back down for more. This constant, well-organized, and harmonious back-and-forth process seemed like a beautifully choreographed dance.

Amos looked up and saw the Lady in White. He had already seen her in the form of a little girl and an old lady. Now she was a young woman, as beautiful as dawn. Her white dress sparkled with light and appeared to float around her. On her head was a crown representing a swan. The Lady in White glided toward Amos and caressed his long hair.

"Amos Daragon, young mask wearer, I did not expect you to arrive so early," she said, smiling. "I chose you for your courage, and I can see that I was not mistaken. I am the mother of all the gods and all the creatures living on Earth. I created the world and I chose you to bring equilibrium back to it. You are still young and have much more to learn. The gods, my children, set a trap to be rid of you. This big war of the divinities saddens me, but I decided not to intervene directly in the course of affairs. I've come to lend you my support in the next test that you will meet. Soon you will bite into the apple of light and become one of these divinities. This will cause a terrible disruption on Earth. Millions of men, women, and creatures of all kinds will die. The world of the living will cross that of the dead."

She smiled again. "You are an open book, Amos, and I can read your intentions. You want to use your divine powers to stabilize the forces of light and dark, but you have to know that it will be difficult for you to do so. I have faith in you, and my thoughts will be with you. Do not renounce who you are for power, and always think of others before thinking of yourself. Until we meet again, young mask wearer."

With these words, the Lady in White vanished. Amos walked slowly toward one of the fruits. He extended his hand to pick the "key" of Braha. The fruit was transparent and extraordinarily luminous. Amos brought it to his mouth and sank his teeth into it.

# —18—

## GOD DARAGON

A terrible explosion shook the Mahikui desert. The top of the pyramid that stuck out of the sand was blown away by the blast. A powerful ray of light coming from the ground pierced the clouds, to fade away in the cosmos. Hundreds of thousands of specters, mummies, skeletons, and other ghosts began to come out of the hole to invade Earth. Yaune the Purifier, still busy fighting Kur, lifted his head.

"My army has arrived at last!" he shouted.

Kur tried to flee. But it was too late for Baron Samedi's dragon. Yaune, now a lich, ordered his soldiers to attack the beast of fire. Kur was rapidly assailed by a horde of specters that struck the beast from all sides and threw it to the ground. At Yaune's request, the dragon's body was carefully examined for the missing scale. He was quickly informed of the dragon's weak spot.

The knight, half dead but still invested with Seth's power, climbed over the beast. He put the tip of his sword against the nape of the monster's neck and raised his arm in a sign of victory.

"Seth! New monarch of the world, here is my first offering to your greatness," Yaune declared solemnly in front of the fast-growing army. "The Elders will never be born again. Let this sacrifice mark the first day of your reign! You have vanquished the pantheon of goodness! Let darkness invade Earth! The world is mine! The world is ours!"

Yaune plunged his sword into the dragon's nape. Kur let out a piercing cry and the mountains sent the echo back over the whole planet. Yaune's army of specters struck up a lugubrious hymn to death. The dragon's body decomposed rapidly, and soon, under the lich's magic, its skeleton took life. Yaune now had a mount worthy of him.

Riding the bones of the monster, Seth's servant rose in the air. He waved his arm and ordered his troops to line up in twos. The ghosts obeyed. Flying over them at high speed, Yaune watched with contentment as the greatest army of the world started its march. A huge part of the desert was now covered with his soldiers. They were everywhere!

"Onward!" Yaune shouted excitedly.

Amos woke up amid a restful white light that was coming from his body. He had tasted the fruit of the tree of life. He had knowledge beyond human understanding, which made life on Earth seem like an ordeal to him. He had never felt so good, so calm, and so sure of himself. Now Amos belonged to the world of the invisible and of eternity. At present, he belonged to a higher level of life, capable of causing volcanic eruptions, of making flowers grow, of creating the race of his choice on Earth. In the blink of an eye, he was able to access the past and the future. He was stronger than a dragon and wiser than wisdom itself.

Amos saw the world's destiny. He saw Yaune's grand quest, the death of millions of humans, and Seth's new reign. Curiously enough, he did not mind so much. The world would live in darkness for thousands of years before being reborn to light. The mask wearer knew this; it was only a matter of time. He would try to thwart Seth's plans. He would raise a large army of his own, made up of strong knights, to fight the specters. His destiny was clear to him now. He would become the new great god of this world and millions of faithful believers would pray to him every night.

There would be temples to celebrate his cult and mantras to glorify his power. Beorf, Junos, and his parents, Frilla and Urban, were no longer on his mind. Amos had forgotten all he knew about his humanity. His only dream was to become mankind's new light, the shining star that would guide it to peace.

An old man appeared in the white space that surrounded Amos. He had a long braided beard. His hair, gathered in a massive pile atop his head, seemed just as long. Deeply wrinkled and stooped under the weight of his years, he held a big book in his hand. He sat in front of Amos and opened the yellowed pages.

"Good day, good afternoon, good night, whatever!" the old man declared in a neutral voice. "I've come to inform you of the different articles linked to the access to divinity. Do not interrupt me while I read. Hold your questions till I am finished."

Amos nodded and the old man went on.

"Article One: He who achieves the rank of the divine must swear allegiance to good or evil. He will be allowed to remain neutral for a thousand years if he so wishes, but he will have to inform me of his choice at the end of this period.

"Article Two: He who becomes divine will have the right to create a new race of mortals if he so wishes. He will also have the right to court a race already in existence that still has no god to glorify. He will have the right to divert worshippers from other gods and thus unify several races of mortals within his own cult. The means used to reach this end are, and will remain, at his discretion. I will provide you with a list of godless people.

"Article Three: He who becomes divine will oversee and be responsible for a portion of the world not yet governed. I will give you a list of vacant domains that I hope will motivate you in your new duties. Do you have any questions? If not, sign here and we will go to the articles linked to your immortality."

The words of the Lady in White came back to Amos. She had said: "Do not renounce who you are for power, and always think of others before thinking of yourself." Inspired by these words, Amos knew what he had to do.

"What if I don't sign?" he asked calmly.

"That will mean you refuse your divine status," the old man answered. "You will be sent back to Earth to live as a simple mortal. No one has ever refused such an offer, but the choice is yours."

"Well," Amos said, "I want to become human again. I know how to restore equilibrium to the world and how to correct my mistakes."

"Beware," the old man said. "As soon as you become human again, you will forget everything about your stay in Braha, the tree of life, and our meeting. All this will be wiped from your memory."

"I'll take the chance. May I just ask for a bit of your pen's ink?"

Puzzled by this request, the old man handed his inkwell to Amos, who promptly drank half of it. He then gargled at length and spat out the black liquid.

"I'm ready!" he said. "I want to go back to Earth exactly one week before the eclipse of the moon that will happen over the realm of Berrion. Is it possible?"

"You are a god. You can do anything! The only trouble

you'll have going back home is that the ink has stained your teeth. I doubt that your teeth will become white again before a long time has passed. But that is your problem! Good luck, young man! When you're ready, close your eyes and express your wish to become human again and things will take their course. Farewell."

The old man disappeared quickly in the surrounding whiteness.

Amos closed his eyes. "I want to wake up in Berrion, the very morning Lolya arrived at Junos's," he said. "I want to wake up in Berrion, the very morning Lolya arrived at Junos's. I want to wake up in Berrion, the very . . ."

# THE NEW AWAKENING

On a cool September morning, Amos was sleeping peace-fully in his room when Beorf rushed in.

"Get up, Amos! Lord Junos wants to see you in the castle courtyard," the plump boy said. "Quick! Hurry, it's important!"

Hardly awake, Amos got up and dressed in a jiffy. Strangely enough, he was sore all over. His arms and legs hurt terribly. He felt as though he had dreamed nonstop for weeks. He combed his hair, put his wolf's-head earring on, and adjusted the black leather armor that his mother had made for him. He stopped abruptly as he was leaving his room. He had the strange sensation that he had already lived through this moment.

*I come out of my room every morning,* he thought, *this is*

167

*nothing unusual. What's more, Junos is an early riser and he often makes me get out of bed in a hurry. So why do I have the feeling that I'm headed toward something ominous?*

The sun had just risen when Amos arrived in the interior courtyard of the castle. All the staff was gathered, waiting impatiently for the young mask wearer. The inquisitive crowd had formed a circle around something or someone. The cooks were talking among themselves in hushed voices, while the guards, the knights, and the archers of the realm were at their lookout posts. The grooms seemed hypnotized and the maids were shaking and looking at one another anxiously. Once more, Amos felt certain he had lived through this exact scene. He looked at the light of day that was slowly taking hold of the place. Maybe he had seen all this in a dream. The discussions he heard and the energy of this gathering vaguely reminded him of something. But what was it? He racked his brain but couldn't come up with anything.

Beorf was already on the central dais, right by Junos's side. The lord of Berrion seemed anxious in his nightgown. His yellow and green nightcap made him look silly, a little like an old clown. But all eyes were on the center of the square. Amos easily forced his way through the compact crowd. His parents, Frilla and Urban Daragon, saw their son join Junos and Beorf on the dais. There again, the feeling of having lived this before filled Amos. It was as if he could predict what was going to happen.

At the center of the gathering, about twenty men were standing proudly, their backs straight, perfectly still. Their skin was as dark as night and their bodies were covered with brightly colored war paint. These warriors from an unknown place were wearing large jewels made of gold, precious stones, and animal bones. They were lightly dressed in animal skins that displayed their powerful muscles and their battle scars. These men with bloodshot eyes and pointed teeth carried powerful spears on their backs. Five black panthers were resting by their side, tongues dangling. Amos had already seen them. All this was familiar to him. He did not move, just carefully observed the group of warriors.

"So, my friend," Junos said as he turned toward Amos. "You seem dazed. Are you not awake? I made you get up in haste because these visitors want to see you. They arrived at the doors of the city this morning asking for you. They are probably demons, be very careful! Look at the size of their cats. They are huge!"

Amos looked at his old friend. "If things take a bad turn," he muttered, "the knights are ready to attack. At the slightest sign of hostility, they will send these men back to hell."

"How strange!" Junos exclaimed. "That's exactly what I was going to say. Since when do you read my thoughts, young mask wearer?"

*Since this morning,* Amos answered to himself.

Amos turned to Beorf and gave him a quick nod. Beorf knew what was expected of him. He stepped down from the dais, staying one step behind Amos, ready to morph into a bear and spring into action.

"I am the one you want to see," Amos said to the visitors.

The warriors looked at one another and made way for him. Everyone then saw a young girl at the center of the gathering. No one had noticed her so far, but the young mask wearer had known she was there, protected by her men. She moved toward Amos with dignity. Her skin too was the color of ebony. Her hair, very long and braided in hundreds of plaits, almost reached the ground. She wore sumptuous gold jewels around her neck, waist, wrists, and ankles. Large bracelets, beautiful and finely intertwined belts, necklaces, and many earrings of different shapes gave her a regal allure. She was magnificent. An elongated jewel pierced her nose between her nostrils. She wore a black fur cape and a leopard-skin dress that left her belly button uncovered. Her navel was pierced as well, with a jewel made of a gold-inlaid green stone.

Amos could not stop staring at one of her earrings—a jewel that he was convinced was in his mouth. Why and how had it gotten there? He could not remember. The girl stopped in front of him and looked him straight in the eyes.

"I am Lolya, queen of the Dogon tribe," she announced.

"I set off on a very long journey from my native land to come and meet you. Baron Samedi, my god and spiritual guide, appeared to me and ordered me to bring you a gift."

The queen snapped her fingers. One of the warriors came forward and placed a wooden box at the girl's feet. Amos knew that a mask of fire was in the box, fire being one of the elements indispensable to his powers. The girl opened the box with care. The crowd overcame their fear and drew closer to see the mysterious gift.

"Take it!" Lolya declared, bowing respectfully. "This object is now yours!"

Just as Amos had thought, the box contained the mask of fire. He raised his head and smiled nervously at Lolya. She burst out laughing.

"My skin is black and my teeth are white," she said, "and your skin is white and your teeth are black. How strange!"

Amos didn't know why, but he knew exactly what he had to do.

"Seize these men!" he shouted at the top of his voice.

The knights immediately threw themselves on the Dogons and immobilized them. Surprised by this sudden attack, the warriors did not have time to resist.

"The girl, Beorf, tackle her!" Amos shouted to his friend.

Beorf fell onto Lolya as fast as lightning. He pinned her to the ground before she could use her magic.

"Let me go, mortals, or you will pay dearly!" a deep and

hollow voice shouted. It was coming from the girl's throat but did not sound like her.

Quickly, Amos bent over Lolya. With one hand, he exerted strength on her lower jaw. Keeping her mouth open, he dipped his other hand down her throat, where he felt a hard and round object. In a quick motion, he slipped his fingers around the object and pulled it out. The crowd was able to see that Amos was holding a red stone. Lolya howled and passed out.

"What is going on, Amos? Who are they?" Junos asked, bewildered. "And what is this stone?"

"I don't know how to explain this, Junos. I don't know how to answer the questions that everyone may have," Amos said cautiously. "I followed my instinct and I still don't know if I did the right thing. Do I really have black teeth?"

"They look stained," Beorf answered. He had regained his human form. "Open your mouth! Yes, your teeth and your gums are completely black."

"This is strange," Amos went on. "As soon as Lolya mentioned my teeth, I knew what I had to do. The stone that I retrieved from her mouth is a draconite. Lolya would have become a dragon if I had not removed it. I think I have prevented a terrible catastrophe. It is Baron Samedi, the one she calls her spiritual guide, who trapped her, by putting the draconite in her throat."

"But how do you know all this?" Junos insisted. "And why are your teeth stained?"

"I don't have the slightest idea," Amos answered with a shrug. "On the other hand, I know exactly what to do with this stone."

Amos took the mask. Made of gold, it represented the face of a man with a beard and mane of hair in the shape of flames. Amos set the stone into it. Then he put the mask over his face. Under everyone's eyes, the gold mask blended over his own face. Suddenly Amos's feet burst into flames. Whispers of alarm rose from the crowd. The flames spread slowly up from his ankles to the tips of his fingers while spiraling around his body. Junos shouted orders to his servants, who threw buckets of water over Amos, to no avail. Amos was still burning.

Amos raised his arms. "Do not worry. The mask is now part of my body. We are becoming one!"

After a few minutes of intense combustion, the fire began to lose its force. The flames died one after the other. The mask had completely disappeared into Amos's face.

"Well, Amos, you told me how you integrated the mask of air over your face," Junos said, "but I had difficulty imagining such a thing. Now I understand!"

"There are four masks," Amos answered. "My face melded with the mask of air during our first adventure; now I possess that of fire. I still have to find the mask of water and the mask of earth. I must also look for the power stones that will increase my control over each element."

As he looked around him, Amos thought he recognized one of the cooks. He walked toward him.

"I know that you are an informer paid by one of our enemies," he said. "You are to meet him soon, are you not?"

The cook fell to his knees. "Yes, you're right. Don't hurt me!" he begged. "Yaune the Purifier wants to set a trap for Junos and asked me to inform him if the lord was to leave Berrion. He promised me a lot of gold. Please don't hurt me. I will tell you where I was to meet him. I will tell you everything!"

"Very well," Amos said as he turned to Junos. "It's our turn to set a trap for him!"

The cook went into the clearing. He was rubbing his hands nervously and perspiring abundantly. Yaune the Purifier appeared on his large red horse, dismounted quickly, and came slowly toward the spy. His shield was decorated with huge snake heads. He removed his helmet. He still had a long scar on his cheek and the word "murderer" tattooed on his forehead.

"Give me what you promised and I'll tell you what you want to know," the cook said.

"Quiet, miserable louse!" Yaune replied nastily. "I'll pay you once you tell me what I want to hear."

"In that case, you won't be dealing with me but rather with him," the cook answered, pointing his finger at the end of the clearing.

In the morning light, Amos appeared in the company of Beorf and Lolya.

"It's time to surrender," Amos shouted. "The men of Berrion have surrounded the clearing. You are trapped."

"Amos Daragon? Is that really you? You're supposed to be dead! You cannot be here!"

"As you can see, I am here! I order you for the last time: surrender!"

Yaune mounted his horse quickly and rushed full speed toward Amos. At this point, Junos's knights came out of the forest. Amos signaled to them to halt. Then he closed his eyes and raised his hand in the direction of his enemy. Immediately, Yaune felt a strong wave of heat engulf him. His armor grew warmer. The horse—its skin in direct contact with the armor—reared up and violently threw its rider off. Yaune hit the ground with a thud. Stunned by his fall, he got up and began to insult heaven and earth. The burns caused by his own armor were unbearable, so he removed it as fast as he could. He ended up nearly naked, which made Junos's men laugh heartily. His pride wounded, Yaune again ran toward Amos, fists and teeth clenched.

Beorf morphed into bear form and rushed at Yaune. The humanimal jumped and collided full speed with the knight. Yaune fell to the ground, giving Beorf enough time to grab Yaune's neck between his teeth.

"Look, this is not right!" Yaune cried, softening his attitude. "I already paid my debt to you. I've been condemned to wander! I've been branded like cattle! Let me go!"

Amos and Lolya approached him.

"You will never leave us in peace," the mask wearer

began. "Your thirst for vengeance is all-consuming and blinds you. I have been chosen to bring equilibrium back to this world—for this reason, you have to be stopped!"

"What will you do? Kill me? Put me in prison, maybe?" Yaune asked.

"No," Amos answered calmly. "If we imprison you, you will probably find a way to escape. Besides, there is no jail in Berrion. We will not kill you, either."

"In that case," Yaune said, laughing, "you cannot do anything against me!"

Amos smiled and asked Lolya to come forward. The young girl bent over the knight. She was holding a chicken under her arm. Junos and his men had encircled their enemy and lit a dozen candles. Lolya began to dance around the knight as she chanted strange incantations. The Dogon warriors formed a circle around them, the rhythm of their drums accompanying their young queen's dance. Yaune could only watch, dumbfounded, as Lolya grabbed his soul and switched it for that of the hen. The queen of the Dogons then asked Beorf to free the man.

The knight got up immediately and began to cackle. He looked nervously around him, then fled flapping his arms, scared by the laughter of the crowd.

"Well, Amos!" Lolya said, exhausted but happy. "Here's one who will never hurt anyone again! If you wish, I can give you the hen. Always keep it in a cage, though, as it surely will be bad-tempered!"

"Thank you," Amos answered, laughing. "It will stay in the large Berrion henhouse. You can be sure that we will never eat its eggs!"

"I thank you for all you did for me," the young queen added. "You freed me of the draconite and now I can return to my country. My people are saved! The Dogons owe you a lot. I will always be there for you if you need me. My powers and magic are at your disposal."

"So!" Amos said with joy. "Let's go back to Berrion! You have to rest before starting your trip home. We will celebrate our victory!"

"And I hope there will be a large feast!" yelled a famished Beorf.

"We will feed you so well that you will explode, Beorf!" Junos told him with a friendly pat on the shoulder.

The happy group began their trip. At the beginning of this new day, Amos, Beorf, Junos, and the men of Berrion went back to their city singing.

# −20−

## THE DRACONITE

In a large forest in the northern country, a little girl was crying bitterly. She was lost and desperate. Her parents had sent her out to collect wood for cooking dinner. The sun was setting and the howling of the wolves was getting dangerously near. The little girl, as blond as a ray of sun, was shivering. Her blue eyes tried to penetrate the darkness of the forest, which was getting more and more opaque. Her dress, torn by the branches, let the autumn cold go through. Leaves of many different colors were falling, creating a thick carpet under her feet.

And then, between the branches, the little girl saw the silhouette of a man. He was emaciated and his eyes shone like burning fires. Long and thin, he wore a top hat, and his skin was the color of burgundy. A black leather coat covered his body. He stopped the young girl with his cane, which had a knob in the shape of a dragon's head.

"Are you lost, little fairy of the woods?" the strange man asked with fatherly concern.

The little girl nodded.

"Well, it's your lucky day. Let me introduce myself. I am Baron Samedi, and soon I'll be your best friend. Come and let me tell you a story."

The little girl was so happy to find help in the forest that she did not resist.

"Don't be afraid of the wolves, my sweet, I'm stronger than they are," the baron went on, smiling a sinister grin. "You're safe now! Listen to my story . . ."

The baron took a red stone out of his coat and pushed it into the child's mouth. The stone set deeply in her throat.

"In ancient times, magnificent creatures peopled Earth," the satisfied god went on. "These big and powerful animals were the masters of this world for centuries. They slept over gigantic treasures in the depth of mountains. One day, because of men's greed, these fantastic animals disappeared from Earth. I've chosen you to become the first of the grand dragons to be born again on every continent, the world over. I had put my hopes in another young girl, but she went astray. I wanted a black dragon, but instead I'll have a magnificent golden and blue-eyed animal!"

The young girl, now under Baron Samedi's influence, held him tight and kissed him on the cheek. Overjoyed, the god kept on talking tenderly to her, stroking her long curly hair.

"Now you no longer have a family. I am your father, your mother, your spiritual guide, your present, and your future! You will become the most beautiful dragon, the most powerful creature of this world. In a while, your body will change! You will be able to fly long distances, eat entire flocks of sheep, and enjoy destroying all villages on your way."

The little girl raised her head. "Will I be able to take revenge on my elder brother, who is always bullying me?" she asked.

The baron burst out laughing, exposing his straight and gleaming teeth.

"You will begin by avenging yourself over him and then you will avenge yourself over the race of men," he answered her. "Together we shall climb on the grand throne of this world and govern all terrestrial creatures. You will be much better than Lolya! By the way, what is your name, little angel?"

"My name is Brising!"

"That's a pretty name! When you become a dragon, I shall give you a new name. You will be called Ragnarok!"

"What does that mean?" Brising asked, curious.

"It means 'gods' twilight,'" the baron answered gently. "With you, the world will know darkness before being reborn in light."

Upon these words, Brising and the baron disappeared into the forest. Far away, villagers were anxiously calling the lost girl.

# MYTHOLOGICAL LEXICON

## The Gods

**Baron Samedi:** In the Haitian tradition of voodoo, Baron Samedi is one of the guardians of the way that leads to the world of the dead. He always wears a top hat and carries a cane.

**Forseti:** The Nordic god of justice. He lives in a palace filled with imposing columns of red gold, with a roof covered in silver. From this dwelling, he passes judgments and arbitrates.

**Lady in White:** A woman of legends and tales found in many different cultures, the Lady in White helps humans accomplish their destiny.

**Seth:** In Egyptian mythology, Seth is the god of darkness and evil. The Egyptians linked him to the desert and often represented him as a man with a monstrous head. He is also linked to crocodiles and animals of the desert.

## Creatures of Legend

**Angels:** Angels are important creatures in Judeo-Christian religions. They are always winged and are the same size as humans. The most important ones are Michael, the chief of celestial armies, and Gabriel, who is associated with the Annunciation, the Resurrection, and death. For Muslims, Gabriel is the angel of truth.

**Charon:** Also known as the ferryman in Greek mythology, Charon ferries the condemned dead across the Styx to hell. Charon only takes aboard those who have been properly buried according to the Greek ways and customs. Passengers are required to pay him a boarding fee.

**Demons:** There are hundreds of demons in all mythologies of the world. Demons are symbols of evil and viciousness.

**Dragons:** According to legends, dragons dwell in caves and can easily live more than four hundred years. The size of elephants, dragons lived in Europe, the Middle East, Central Asia, India, and Southeast Asia.

**Guédés:** In Haitian voodoo tradition, guédés are the spirits of death. They are associated with the decaying of bodies and with the renewal of life. They are mocking and irreverent.

**Humanimals:** Humanimals are present in the culture of every country. The werewolf is one of the most famous of these creatures. Sometimes kind, sometimes menacing, humanimals are divided into races and species. The full moon often plays an important role in the transformation of a human into an animal.

**Lichs:** Lichs are immortal—the most powerful of all the living dead because they possess potent magical powers.

They appear as skeletons and always wear gold crowns as a sign of their majesty.

**The Phooka:** The Phooka is an Irish goblin that can take several animal forms. Its eyes are sparkling and it is often completely black. More than anything, it loves to transform itself into a pony so it can take a passenger for a ride and send him into a ditch after the hellish outing.

**The Styx:** The origin of this river, also called the river of hatred, is uncertain. It separates the world of the living and that of the dead. In Greek mythology the Styx supposedly turns nine times around the tower of Hades (or hell) before it disappears into the void.

## ABOUT THE AUTHOR

**Bryan Perro** (bryanperro.com) completed training as an actor and a drama teacher at the University of Québec in Montréal and obtained a master's degree in Québec Studies at the University of Québec in Trois-Rivières. He achieved his dream of becoming a full-time writer thanks to his bestselling twelve-book children's series, Amos Daragon, which won the Québécois Children's Science Fiction and Fantasy Award. Recognized internationally, the series has been translated into eighteen languages. Bryan Perro lives in Saint-Mathieu-du-Parc, Québec, Canada.